The Mystery of the

Two-Toed Pigeon

Jupiter switched on the tape of the Investigators' answering machine.

"Help!" Maureen Melody's voice said. "I need your help!" The eccentric bird lover was almost singing in her agitation.

"There's a murderer at large! I went out and found his poor dead body—"

Her voice faltered as she choked back a sob.

"Please help me," she managed to wail. "Somebody's murdering my birds!"

The Three Investigators in

The Mystery of the

Two-Toed Pigeon

by Marc Brandel

Based on characters created by
Robert Arthur

RANDOM HOUSE 🏠 NEW YORK

Library of Congress Cataloging in Publication Data:

Brandel, Marc
  The Three Investigators in
The mystery of the two-toed pigeon.
  (The Three Investigators mystery series; no. 37)
  "Based on characters created by Robert Arthur."
  SUMMARY: A pigeon with a missing toe leads three young
sleuths to a group of ingenious thieves.
  [1. Mystery and detective stories] I. Title. II. Series.
PZ7.B7362Thr   1984   [Fic]   83-21174
ISBN: 0-394-85976-6 (pbk.); 0-394-95976-0 (lib. bdg.)

Manufactured in the United States of America
   3 4 5 6 7 8 9 0

Contents

Introduction

by Hector Sebastian

Hello, my name's Hector Sebastian.

I'm a writer by profession. I write mystery stories and some of them have been made into movies.

But I'm not here to talk about myself. I only felt I should tell you I was a mystery writer because I think it's one of the reasons I am always so interested in the mysterious adventures of three young friends of mine.

They don't get involved in the adventures by accident. At least not entirely by accident. Take this latest adventure of theirs, which they call the Mystery of the Two-Toed Pigeon. It did all start with a strange, chance meeting. But if they hadn't been the kind of boys they are, they would have left it at that and forgotten the whole thing.

Except that they didn't. They spotted a mystery and they kept trying to puzzle it out. They kept following up odd clues, putting themselves into some pretty dangerous situations. That's the way they are.

They call themselves The Three Investigators. Let me tell you a little about them.

Their names are Jupiter Jones, Pete Crenshaw, and Bob Andrews. They live in Rocky Beach, a small city on the coast of southern California, a few miles from Santa Monica.

Jupiter Jones, usually known as Jupe, is the leader of the three. He is short and . . . well, not exactly plump. Tubby? I guess the word he would choose for himself would be stocky. He has a remarkable memory, a quick deductive mind, and unusual powers of observation. These qualities and an unshakable determination to get to the bottom of anything make him an excellent investigator.

There are people, I guess, who think Jupe has his faults too. But he's not really conceited. He just seems rather sure of himself. And he has reason to be. If he thinks he's right about something, he usually is.

Pete Crenshaw, the Second Investigator, is tall and rangy. A natural athlete, he likes baseball and swimming and bicycling. He has a great affection for animals, a good sense of humor, and a lot more humility than Jupe. He is more cautious too. He doesn't believe in sticking his neck out, although, as you will see, he sometimes finds he has to.

Bob Andrews, the Third Investigator, is in charge of records and research. He is intelligent and studious and a little shy. He usually carries a notebook with him and writes down things he sees and hears in a special shorthand he made up. I think he'll probably turn out to be a newspaperman one day.

So now that you know who the Three Investigators are, I'll shut up and let you meet them for yourselves. You'll meet some other unusual people in this story too. That's a promise!

HECTOR SEBASTIAN

The Mystery of the

Two-Toed Pigeon

1

The Winking Man

"I vote we stop at the diner for a hamburger," Pete Crenshaw called back to the other two boys.

It was the beginning of summer vacation. The Three Investigators, Jupiter Jones, Bob Andrews, and Pete, had spent most of the day swimming at their favorite beach. Now they were biking home along the ocean highway to Rocky Beach, a small coastal city in southern California several miles from Santa Monica.

Bob agreed to a burger at once, quickening his speed to catch up with Pete.

Jupiter Jones, the First Investigator, considered the suggestion in his usual methodical way. On the one hand he was hot and tired—he had never enjoyed physical exertion much; he preferred to use his brain—and the idea of stopping at the old Seahorse Diner at the top of the next hill was very appealing.

On the other hand Jupiter was rather . . . heavy for his height. He had even heard one or two boys in school refer to him as fat. And he had made up his mind to do something about that this summer, to lose at least five pounds before school started again in September.

Laboring up the hill, he explored the question of a burger a little further. It was three o'clock, six hours since breakfast. He had been swimming, he had cycled several miles, he had burned up a considerable number of calories. . . . And besides, he was hungry.

"Okay," he shouted ahead to the other two boys. "Let's pull in at the Seahorse."

The diner was almost empty at that time in the afternoon. The Three Investigators found a booth near the window overlooking the highway. Pete sprawled comfortably in his seat. Bob studied the menu.

The First Investigator was alertly watching the few other people in the diner. He was pursuing his favorite hobby, trying to deduce what he could about people from their faces, the way they were dressed, their behavior.

One man in particular aroused his interest. He was thin and rather short, about five feet five. He was wearing a dark suit, a white shirt open at the neck, and pointed black shoes. He had surprisingly large feet for his height. From the racing form stuck in his pocket, Jupe could guess he was a horseplayer, a gambler.

As the man sat at the counter with a cup of coffee in front of him, he kept swiveling on his stool and glancing nervously through the window at the highway. Every time he did this he would reach out with his hand and clasp the large square box on the stool beside him, as though to make sure it was still there. The box was wrapped in cheesecloth, neatly taped at the corners.

Jupiter turned his head slightly so that he could see the passing traffic while still watching the small man in the dark suit out of the corner of his eye.

Several limousines sped almost silently past. The man paid no attention to them. Then Jupe heard the louder, more grinding sound of another motor approaching. The small man leaped off his stool and stood staring at the window with alert, waiting eyes. A camper came into sight. The man sat down again.

The man must be watching for a heavy vehicle, a van or a truck, Jupe reasoned, but not a camper.

The waitress brought their hamburgers. Jupe took off the top half of his bun and put it to one side. That way he would be cutting down his intake of starches. He glanced at the man in the dark suit again. For a moment their eyes met.

Then an odd thing happened. The man winked at him. Jupe found himself smiling back.

The man seemed to take that as an invitation. Hugging his square box, he approached the booth where the Three Investigators were sitting.

"You boys been swimming?" The question was just a friendly one, but the man's way of asking seemed to give it a special secret meaning. Because as soon as the man had spoken, he winked again.

"Yeah," Pete told him, grinning with his mouth full of hamburger. "Up at Wills Beach."

"Wills Beach, huh?" the man echoed him. "No wonder you're hungry."

Wink.

There was nothing particularly funny about the remark. But the Three Investigators couldn't help laughing. No matter what the man said, the wink at the end made it sound like the punch line of a joke.

The man smiled back at them.

"Mind if I join you?" he asked.

Wink.

Jupe slid closer to the window and the man sat next to him, putting his cloth-covered box on the floor beside him.

"My name's Stan," he said, giving them another suggestive wink with his right eye. The three boys introduced themselves: "Jupe," "Pete," "Bob."

"Glad to know you." Jupe couldn't see whether

the man winked at them after saying this. Stan
had jumped out of his seat and was tensely
watching the highway at the sound of another
heavy vehicle approaching. An oil truck passed.
Stan sat down again.

"Stan. Short for Stanley," he went on after a
moment. "But everyone calls me Blinky. I guess
you can see why."

Although he winked again after saying this,
none of the boys felt like laughing this time. They
realized that the constant winking of Stan's right
eye was involuntary. He didn't mean anything by
it. He just couldn't help it. It was a nervous tic.

Bob felt rather sorry for him in a friendly way.
The Three Investigators all felt even more
friendly toward him when he called over the
waitress and handed her a ten-dollar bill.

"It's my treat," he told her.

Wink.

"I'm paying for the whole party. Okay?"

Wink.

The waitress put her hands on her hips and
scowled at him. She was probably tired of
customers getting fresh with her. Then she
nodded and took the money and walked back to
the counter.

The three boys thanked Blinky for his
kindness. For a few minutes there was no sound of
approaching trucks and everyone relaxed. Jupe
had finished his hamburger and was feeling

pleased with himself for leaving half of his bun uneaten. It made him feel like showing off a little.

"Do you like living in Santa Monica?" he asked Blinky.

Blinky straightened abruptly in his seat. His hand shot out and clasped the box beside him. For several seconds his right eyelid opened and closed like the shutter of a movie camera.

"How did you know where I live?" he asked hoarsely.

Jupiter hadn't meant to startle the man. He smiled at him reassuringly. "It's just a game I play," he explained. "There were only three cars in the parking lot when we arrived. One of them had a teddy bear lying on the front seat, so I figured it must belong to that lady over there, the one with the little girl. The second one had a surfboard tied to the roof." The First Investigator indicated a well-built young man with sun-bleached hair sipping a Coke at the counter. "He's the only person here who looks like a surfer," he pointed out. "The third car had a Santa Monica dealer's name under the license plate, so I just figured it must be yours."

Blinky stared at him for a moment in silence.

"I see," he said. "This game. It's sort of like you're playing detective."

"Well, we don't just play at that." Jupiter wasn't exactly offended. He simply felt he owed it to himself and Pete and Bob to make clear who they were. "We are detectives. We're The Three Investigators."

He slipped a card from his shirt pocket and handed it to Blinky. He had printed it himself on an old press that his uncle Titus had bought as junk for his salvage yard. On the card it said:

THE THREE INVESTIGATORS
"We Investigate Anything"
?   ?   ?
First Investigator . . . . . Jupiter Jones
Second Investigator . . . . Pete Crenshaw
Records and Research . . . Bob Andrews

Under that was the private phone number of their headquarters in the junkyard.

Blinky read the card carefully.

"What are the question marks for?" he asked.

"They stand for mysteries unsolved, riddles unanswered," Jupe told him.

"They're sort of our private trademark," Bob explained.

Blinky nodded and winked as he put the card away in his pocket.

"Do you get many—" he began.

He never finished the sentence. Jupe never knew whether he was going to say "many mysteries" or "inquiries" or "clients." Blinky was on his feet again, staring out the window. Jupe heard the distant, grinding sound of a faltering motor. He saw a green van as it came up the hill toward the diner and rattled past. The driver looked Japanese.

Jupiter turned to glance at Blinky. But the little man in the dark suit was no longer there. He was halfway to the door. In an instant he was through it and racing across the parking lot.

Pete was the first to react. As an athlete he had faster reflexes than the others. He snatched up the square box from the floor beside the booth and hurried after the fleeing Blinky.

"Hey, wait," he shouted. "You forgot . . ."

But he was too late to catch him. As Pete ran across the parking lot, Blinky's two-door black sedan screeched onto the highway and roared off after the green van.

Pete walked back into the diner and put the large square box on their table.

The Three Investigators sat in silence and looked at it.

Jupe was pinching his lower lip in the way he did when he was thinking hard. He claimed that it helped him concentrate.

Bob spoke first. "We'd better give it to the waitress," he said. "Blinky's sure to come back here looking for it."

Pete agreed that that was a sensible suggestion, but the First Investigator just kept pinching his lip. Blinky himself, and the little man's excitement at the sight of the green van, had fired his curiosity. Jupe's naturally inquiring mind couldn't bear to leave any puzzle unsolved. He felt sure the Three Investigators were faced with what promised to be an intriguing mystery.

"I vote we take the box back to Headquarters," he said. "And look after it for Blinky until he gets in touch with us. He's got our card with our phone number and . . ."

He could see that Pete was going to object. The Second Investigator didn't have Jupe's over-developed taste for adventure.

"After all," Jupiter went on quickly, "Blinky didn't leave the box with the waitress, did he? He left it with us. You could even say he entrusted us with it . . ."

"You could also say he was in such a hurry that he forgot it," Pete put in. But he already knew they would go along with Jupe's suggestion. Jupiter was the natural leader of the three. That was why he was the First Investigator.

Half an hour later the boys were back at their headquarters in the Jones Salvage Yard.

Headquarters was a thirty-foot mobile home trailer that Jupe's uncle, Titus Jones, had bought a long time ago and never been able to sell. The boys had gradually piled great heaps of junk around it, until the trailer was completely hidden from the rest of the yard. The boys had their own secret ways of entering it.

Inside was an office with a desk, an old filing

cabinet, and a phone, which they paid for with money they earned doing odd jobs for Jupe's uncle and aunt in the yard.

Pete, who had carried the box back on his bicycle, put it on the desk.

"Okay," he said. "One mysterious box that doesn't belong to us. What do you want to do with it now? Open it?"

Jupe sat down in the swivel chair behind the desk. He shook his head regretfully. "I don't think we have any right to do that," he said. "I'm afraid we'll just have to—"

He broke off. He leaned forward. He put his ear against the cheesecloth that covered the box.

All three of them could hear it now. A soft, fluttering sound. There was something alive and moving there under the cheesecloth.

"Well, we've got no choice now," Pete said. "We'll have to open it."

All his life Pete Crenshaw had had a very strong feeling for animals. Until his mother had finally, firmly put a stop to it, he had been in the habit of bringing home stray cats and dogs, even a horse he had once found wandering along the highway. The idea that there was an animal shut up in the box was not an idea he could live with.

He stepped forward and stripped the tape off the corners of the box. He lifted aside the cheesecloth. Under it was a square metal cage.

Inside the cage was a pigeon.

It was a beautiful bird, sleek and full-feathered, with a great fan of a tail. Dark gray, its plumage had such a high gloss that it seemed to have a blue sheen.

Then Jupiter noticed something else about the bird. One of its toes was missing. The pigeon had three toes on its right foot, but only two toes on its left.

"We can't leave it in a tiny cage like that," Pete said firmly. "If we're going to keep it, and I guess we are, we've got to find a bigger, more comfortable place for it to live in."

Jupe nodded. "Six two-by-fours," he said. "A roll of chicken wire, nails, and a hammer."

Within a few minutes the Three Investigators had found what they needed in the junkyard. Jupe, who was very skillful with his hands, got busy in his outdoor workshop. Soon he had the two-by-fours nailed together into a boxlike frame. Then he rolled and nailed the chicken wire around it and made a safe, large, comfortable house for the pigeon.

Pete brought the bird out of Headquarters while Jupe found a sack of corn that his aunt Mathilda kept for feeding the ducks in the town park. Bob fetched a saucer of fresh water.

"In you go," Pete said, gently releasing the pigeon from its small cage into its new home.

The bird seemed quite happy there. It pecked at the corn, dipped its beak in the water, then after a few fluttering leaps settled down in a corner and tucked its head under its wing. The pigeon seemed to be saying it was time to call it a day.

It was time for the Three Investigators to call it a day too. They left the pigeon in the workshop, out of the way in a front corner of the yard. Bob and Pete cycled off to their own homes, and Jupe walked across the street to the small house where he lived with his aunt and uncle. They had given him a home ever since he was orphaned as a small boy.

Jupe was up early the next morning. Pulling on his clothes, he hurried over to the salvage yard.

The new cage was still there in Jupe's workshop, safely tucked away under the shelter of some corrugated iron roofing. As Jupiter approached the cage, he could see the beautiful sleek gray bird hopping cheerfully about and pecking at its corn.

Jupe knelt down and pressed his face against the chicken wire.

"Where did you come from?" he wondered aloud. "And what was Blinky doing with you in that box? And why was he so nervous?"

There was certainly a mystery about the pigeon, he decided.

And then Jupiter saw that there was even more of a mystery about the bird than he had imagined.

The pigeon he was looking at had three toes on each foot.

2
The Singing Bird Lover

"It's a Belgian Racing Homer," Bob said. "I mean they both are."

Jupe had phoned the other two Investigators as soon as he discovered the new pigeon, but it wasn't till after lunch that all three boys were free to meet at Headquarters.

Bob Andrews, who had spent the morning on his part-time job at the public library in Rocky Beach, had found an illustrated book about pigeons. He showed Jupe and Pete the colored photograph of the Belgian Racing Homer in the book.

Jupe studied it, comparing it to the three-toed pigeon, which now sat on the desk in front of him in the smaller cage.

"Yes, you're right, Bob," he said. "The two birds are identical except for that missing toe on the first one. And they're both racing homers."

He handed the book back to Bob. Pete put the tip of his finger through the bars of the cage and gently stroked the bird's wing feathers. The pigeon seemed to like it. The bird looked at Pete in a bright, expectant way.

"It happens to them fairly often," Pete said. "Haven't you ever noticed? Quite a lot of the wild pigeons on the beaches around here have missing toes."

The First Investigator nodded absently. The truth was he had never paid much attention to pigeons until now, but he saw no reason to admit that to his friends. "They get their feet caught in gratings," he said with assumed authority. "Or have accidents involving other man-made obstacles."

He glanced at Bob, who was deeply absorbed in the pigeon book. "What does it say about Belgian Homers?" he asked.

"They're champion racers. They're bred for it. And the people who breed them and race them—it's like horse trainers—they can recognize and pick out any pigeon among a flock of hundreds."

He read on in silence for a minute, then looked up, settling his glasses on his nose.

"It's incredible," he said. "People take them

from their lofts and transport them in trucks, in wicker baskets or covered cages, sometimes as far as five or six hundred miles. Then they let them go and the birds all race to their own homes. The champions average sixty miles an hour. None of them ever gets lost. They all seem to know the way home at once, no matter where they've been taken to, or where they've come from."

He glanced back at the book. "It's the national sport in Belgium. One time a racing homer was put in a basket in the dark hold of a ship and taken all the way to Indochina. It flew back to Belgium, over seven thousand miles, in twenty-four days. Across totally unfamiliar territory."

"Let me see." Pete reached for the book and studied it for a minute in silence.

"Hey, this is unreal," he said. "Homing pigeons can be messengers. It all goes way back in history. Caesar used pigeon posts in his conquest of Gaul. And the U.S. Army used them for years. As recently as the Korean War. And there used to be a regular pigeon air-mail service between Los Angeles and Catalina Island. Did you know all that, Jupe?"

The First Investigator didn't answer. He was busy pinching his lower lip.

"The question is . . . how?" Jupiter said after a moment. "How? And why?"

"The book says nobody really knows how the

birds can locate their homes," said Bob. He took the book back from Pete. "They've been studying the whole subject at Cornell University and the best guess they've come up with is that it may have something to do with atmospheric pressure. Pigeons are extremely sensitive to atmospheric pressure as well as to sounds. But listen to this. It's some professor talking. 'The only way we could understand the pigeon's homing instinct is by being pigeons ourselves, feeling like pigeons, thinking like pigeons.' "

He looked at the beautiful glossy bird in its small cage, as though trying to understand how it did feel to be a pigeon.

Jupiter shook his head. "I didn't mean how or why do pigeons find their way home," he said. "I meant how did that particular pigeon find its way into the cage we made for Blinky's two-toed bird. Who switched them during the night? How did they know where the two-toed pigeon was? And why did they do it?"

"Beats me." Pete was gently stroking the Belgian Racer again. It cooed softly back at him like a purring cat. "Let's give him a name," Pete suggested. "Let's call him Caesar."

"Possibility number one." The First Investigator was thinking aloud, as he often did when something puzzled him. "Blinky himself switched the birds. He had our card with our names on it ..." Jupe couldn't see any reason for modesty . . . "and we're pretty well known in Rocky Beach. He'd only have to ask anyone where Jupiter Jones lived."

"Well, almost anyone," Pete agreed.

"Possibility number two," Jupe continued. "The man in the green van that Blinky followed. He could have pulled off the road somewhere and seen Pete ride by with that box on his bicycle. He could have trailed us here. Although I must admit I didn't notice him if he did."

Jupiter looked gloomily at the cooing Caesar, as though blaming the bird in some way for his own lack of observation. Then he brightened slightly.

"Blinky and the man in the green van," he said. "What do we know about them? We don't know Blinky's last name or his address, only that he lives in Santa Monica. He pulled out of that parking lot so fast that I only managed to get the letters on his license plate: MOK. The green van's plate was so spattered with mud that I couldn't read it at all. We seem to be at a dead end—except for one thing."

"What?" Pete knew he could think about it for the rest of his life and not catch up with Jupe's reasoning.

"Pigeons. Not just ordinary, run-of-the-mill pigeons. But carefully bred, highly trained racing homers. And that's like horses, as you said, Bob. The people who go in for it all know about each other. There must be some club or association that could tell us who those people are . . ."

He was already reaching for the classified section of the telephone directory.

"And if we can get in touch with some trainer or breeder, he might recognize this bird—"

"Caesar," Pete interrupted him. "His name's Caesar."

"—And tell us who it belongs to."

Jupe was leafing rapidly through the yellow pages. *"P* for pigeon," he muttered. *"A* for association. *C* for club. *A* for Audubon. Um . . ." He was silent for a minute, his eyes darting from page to page.

"And . . ." he said slowly in a disappointed voice, "all that seems to leave is *P* for pet shop."

"Or Miss Melody," Bob suggested.

"Who's Miss Melody?" Jupe raised his eyes from the phone book.

"She's a woman who comes into the library sometimes. All she ever takes out is books about birds. She's crazy about birds. I talked to her once and she told me she was president of a society called Our Feathered Friends."

Jupe closed the directory and put it back on the filing cabinet.

"It's a chance," he said. "If there are any pigeon experts around here, she might know about them. Do you know where she lives?"

"No." Bob took off his glasses and polished them. "Except she must live in Rocky Beach or she couldn't belong to the library. And her full name's Maureen Melody. I remember her library card."

Jupe soon found Maureen Melody in the Rocky Beach phone book. She lived on Alto Drive about two miles away.

"I vote for biking up there," Pete said. "But what will we do with Caesar while we're gone?"

Jupe couldn't see why they shouldn't just leave him where he was in his cage on the desk. But Pete insisted that if Caesar was to be left all alone, they would have to put him back in his bigger cage in the yard.

Jupe shook his head at that. "It's too easy for anyone to steal him there," he said. "Look what happened last night."

"We might even come back and find he'd been switched for a four-toed pigeon," Bob added.

The Three Investigators finally agreed to take Caesar with them. Pete opened the trailer's main exit—a trap door in the floor above a secret tunnel that led into the outdoor workshop. He crawled out, holding the cage against his chest. Bob followed him.

Jupe was about to enter the tunnel too when he paused, frowning. He walked back to his desk and switched on the answering machine attached to the phone. Then he lowered himself through the trap door and closed it after him.

Alto Drive was on the east side of Rocky Beach. The East Side was the Feast Side, Jupe's Uncle Titus had once said. It was a neighborhood of large houses set well back from the road on their own acres of lawns and trees and gardens.

The Three Investigators got off their bicycles outside a pair of tall wrought-iron gates. MELODY NEST, a sign said in curlicue iron letters.

There was a security intercom system set into one of the stone pillars of the gates. Jupe pressed the button and leaned his ear against the answer box above it.

He didn't really expect to hear anything. Ever since the three boys had come within a quarter of a mile of Melody Nest, they had scarcely been able to hear each other. Not even when they shouted.

It was like being in a stereo store, Jupe thought, with every radio and tape deck in the place turned up to full volume. Except that it wasn't music or human voices that filled the air. It was the weirdest mixture of whistles and screeches and cawings he had ever heard.

Jupe pressed the button again. He couldn't hear a sound from the answer box, but a high mocking scream seemed to rend the sky.

He stepped back, looking up into the trees beyond the gates. The red and yellow cockatoo perched among the leaves there mocked him again with its shrill, screeching call.

"Birds!" Pete shouted. "The whole place is full of . . ."

His last word was drowned by a chorus of piercing whistles.

"Birds," Jupe finished for him. He could see them now, or at least some of them. Starlings and sparrows and canaries and larks and crows and hawks and even an eagle, swooping and darting and fluttering through the trees or perched on the branches.

Jupe abandoned the intercom. He had noticed that, although the gates were bolted, there was no padlock on them. He slipped his hand between the bars and pulled back the bolt. Wheeling his bicycle, he walked through the open gates. Pete and Bob followed him, Bob pausing inside to push the bolt back into place.

"What now?" Pete shouted, leaning close to Jupe's ear.

Jupe pointed to the driveway winding away from them into the trees. Still wheeling their bicycles and carrying the caged Caesar, the Three Investigators started up it.

The noise did not decrease as they advanced. It seemed, if possible, to grow even louder. It was all Bob could do not to let go of the handlebars of his bicycle and clasp his hands over his ears.

Jupe, who was leading, halted abruptly. A hundred yards ahead of him, just visible through the trees and the clouds of swooping birds, was a large Spanish-style house. But it wasn't the sight of the house that had made Jupiter stop.

Above all the whistlings and shriekings and cawings he had heard another sound. It was the sound of a woman's voice. A shrill, high, but pleasantly musical soprano. She was singing.

"There are three boys in my driveway, and I wonder what they want," she sang.

Bob recognized the tune of "The Battle Hymn of the Republic."

"They can come a little closer, but they mustn't harm my birds," the voice continued after a moment to the same tune.

The Three Investigators walked on.

Jupe could see the woman now. She was standing on the lawn that divided the house from the trees. She was very tall and what Jupe had heard his English teacher call statuesque. She was wearing a long, full summer dress and a floppy straw hat with a ribbon tied in a bow under her full, rounded chin.

She had a parrot perched on one shoulder and a hawk was hovering just above her head. A canary was comfortably settled on the brim of her hat.

"If you wish to state your business, you will have to sing it loud," she trilled at them as the Three Investigators stopped a few yards from her. "Otherwise I can't hear."

Jupiter Jones had once been a child actor

—although it was not something he cared to be reminded about, since his professional name had been Baby Fatso. But he had never appeared in musicals or joined the school glee club. He had never thought of himself as a singer.

Still, he could see what the woman meant. Among all the chirping and cawing and whistling of the birds, the only human sound that seemed able to reach the ear was a voice raised in song.

"We are looking for the owner, a Miss Maureen Melody," he sang.

"I am the one you're seeking, Maureen Melody herself," she trilled back at him.

It was Jupe's turn again. He cleared his throat.

"We are sorry to intrude here, but we'd like to talk to you." It was difficult to find words that fit the tune of "The Battle Hymn of the Republic," but he was doing his best. "We have heard—"

He broke off. Maureen Melody was evidently no longer listening to him. She was smiling, a wide smile of delight, as she danced forward toward Pete.

"Glory, glory, hallelujah. Glory, glory, hallelujah," she crooned.

She seized the cage with Caesar in it from Pete's handlebars and hugged it against her chest.

"Glory, glory, hallelujah. I'll pay you the reward right now!"

3
Miss Melody
Gets a Pearl

"What reward—?" Jupe started to sing. He stopped. Maureen Melody was opening Caesar's cage.

"Please," he chanted instead. "Please, don't."

As politely as he could he took the cage back from Miss Melody.

"You see, it's not our pigeon," he sang.

He paused again. There was a good deal of explaining to be done and the idea of having to do it all singing at the top of his voice was discouraging. It was more likely to lead to a bad sore throat than to any clear understanding of the situation.

"Is there anywhere we can go where we can talk the whole thing over?" he chanted. It was easier to make up his own tune as he went along than to stick to "The Battle Hymn of the Republic." "Please, I would appreciate it so."

Miss Melody stood, fingering the three ropes of pearls she was wearing and looking at the boys. She seemed a little put out at the way Jupiter had taken Caesar away from her.

Then she nodded and led the way toward the house. The hawk above her head swooped away into the trees. The parrot stayed where it was, on her shoulder. So did the canary, nestling on the brim of her hat.

The Three Investigators followed Miss Melody through tall French windows into a large, light living room. Miss Melody closed the windows after them.

At first the cawing and chirping and whistling from outside seemed almost as deafening as before. Then Miss Melody pressed a button in the wall, and a heavy sheet of plate glass slid into place across the windows.

It was wonderful, Pete thought. Like scuba diving, plunging deep into the ocean. All you could hear was the silence.

"Now won't you let me set that poor bird free?" Maureen Melody said in a normal speaking voice. She stared at Jupe with a reproachful, hurt look in her deep blue eyes. "I thought that was why you had brought him here. I thought you had seen one of my handbills. As founder and president of

Our Feathered Friends, I pay twenty dollars to anyone to free any caged bird. I can't bear to see birds caged. It's so cruel."

"Cruel," the parrot on her shoulder echoed her. "Cruel. Cruel."

At least that cleared up the puzzle of what she had meant about the reward, Jupe thought. Now it was his turn to explain. He began by telling Miss Melody that Caesar didn't belong to them. He had been left in their care by a stranger and they were anxious to return the pigeon to him.

Bob watched Maureen Melody while Jupiter was talking. For all her size, she was a good-looking woman. She reminded him of some former movie star, enormously enlarged on a 3-D screen.

"If we can find Caesar's owner," Pete was saying, "he'll return the bird to his flock. And Caesar is sure to live in a coop or a loft, not a cage."

"I see." Miss Melody was fingering her pearls again. Besides the three strands around her neck, she was also wearing pearl earrings.

"That's why we came to visit you," Bob said. "I knew you were very interested in birds because we talked about it once in the library. And we thought you might know if there's anyone around here who trains and races homing pigeons."

Miss Melody didn't answer. She was staring past him at the window.

"Excuse me," she said. She pressed the button in the wall again. The plate glass slid back. The screeching orchestra filled the room once more.

Miss Melody opened the French windows. There was a bird standing just outside on the path. It was a magpie, Pete saw.

Maureen Melody knelt down and took something from the bird's beak.

"Such a clever friend," she sang in her rich soprano voice, improvising her own tune now. "I call him Edgar Allan Poe. I know Poe's bird was a raven. But I love his poem so. You must have read it. 'Quoth the Raven, Nevermore.' "

The magpie hopped back into the garden and she slid the glass panel closed again.

"Magpies are supposed to be such thieves," she went on in her normal voice. "But my two pet magpies aren't thieves at all. Especially Edgar Allan Poe. He's a wonderful retriever. He's always bringing me things. Lovely things. Look."

She held out her large, plump, white hand, showing the Three Investigators what Edgar Allan Poe had just brought her.

It was a huge, glistening pearl.

"That's the third pearl he's brought me this month," she said. "I can't imagine where he finds them, but I do love pearls so much. Pearls and birds. They're my twin passions."

"About racing pigeons," Jupe reminded her. "Do you happen to know anyone . . ."

Miss Melody shook her head. "I can't think of anyone at the moment, I'm afraid."

"Well, if you do"—Jupe took a Three Investigators card from his pocket and handed it to her—"I'd be very grateful if you'd call us and let us know."

Maureen Melody took the card, but before she could look at it the parrot hopped off her shoulder, seized the card in its beak, and flew over to its perch.

"Thank you for your time," Jupe said to Miss Melody. Although he rather liked the woman, he didn't think they were getting anywhere, and he was beginning to feel a little like a caged bird himself in this soundproof room.

Smiling, Miss Melody opened the panel again and let them out through the French windows. She wasn't smiling at *them,* Jupe noticed, but at the large perfect pearl she was still holding in her hand.

The Three Investigators wheeled their bicycles back down the drive. There was no use trying to talk until they were well clear of Melody Nest, Jupe decided. He trudged ahead through the barrage of bird sounds.

He hadn't gone far when a sudden shrill call stopped him. He thought at first that it was just one of the birds screeching, but when he glanced back at the house he saw Maureen Melody standing there with her hands raised.

"I have a friend," she sang to him. "His name is Parker Frisbee and he lives right here in town. He once told me he raced pigeons. It had slipped my mind."

"Parker Frisbee," Jupe sang back at her. "Thank you!"

4
A Cry for Help

"Parker Frisbee," Jupe repeated when the Investigators were back in the quiet of the highway. "That's the name of that jewelry store on Main Street."

He cycled over to the grass shoulder and dismounted. Bob and Pete joined him.

"You know what I think?" Pete said. "I think Maureen Melody's right. We just ought to let Caesar out of his cage. Let him fly away home and forget the whole thing."

It was exactly what Jupe had been afraid Pete might think. He could see that from Caesar's point of view Pete was probably right. If they opened his cage, Caesar could take off and rejoin his friends in the flock wherever he lived.

But from the First Investigator's point of view, letting Caesar fly away was the worst thing they could do. To Jupe, Caesar was more than a pigeon. He was a clue, the only one they had in what to Jupe was a puzzling and exciting mystery. A case.

He thought of the phone back at Headquarters, the waiting answering machine. If it was the man in the green van who had switched the pigeons the night before, then sooner or later Blinky would call. He would want his two-toed homer back. Jupe wanted to be there when Blinky came for his pigeon. He wanted to watch the little man's face when Blinky saw the three toes on the pigeon's left foot.

He wanted to see if Blinky recognized Caesar.

"I vote we at least go and see Parker Frisbee," the First Investigator said. "It's on our way back to Headquarters anyway."

He looked at Bob, hoping for his support. Bob looked at Pete.

"Okay," Pete agreed reluctantly. "Parker Frisbee, here we come."

Frisbee's was the best, or at least the most expensive, jewelry store in Rocky Beach. Its window wasn't cluttered with watches and engagement rings. There was a single string of pearls on a black velvet stand, flanked by two diamond brooches that sparkled in the sunlight and seemed to say, "You think we're something.

You ought to see what's inside."

Inside were several discreet glass cases containing an assortment of even more expensive-looking jewelry.

A man was standing behind one of the cases. He was short and a little stout and was wearing a black cutaway coat and sharply pressed striped trousers. He was also probably wearing a starched white collar and a silk tie. It was impossible to tell. Whatever he had around his neck was completely hidden by a full black beard. Most of his face was hidden by the beard too. Only his nose and eyes showed like clearings in the forest of hair that covered his chin, his upper lip, and most of both cheeks.

"Yes?" he said when the Three Investigators entered.

"Mr. Parker Frisbee?" Jupe asked.

"Yes."

Jupiter explained that they were friends of Miss Maureen Melody's. Mr. Frisbee's eyes gleamed at the mention of her name. The First Investigator went on to say that Miss Melody had told them Mr. Frisbee was a racing pigeon expert and he wondered if Mr. Frisbee might help them identify a certain Belgian Racing Homer they had found.

"Oh, I'm not really an expert." Mr. Frisbee shrugged modestly. "I did have a few pigeons once and I used to race them in an amateur way. But I gave it up years ago."

He glanced at the cage that Pete was holding. "Is that the bird there?"

"Yes, it is." Pete lifted Caesar so that Mr. Frisbee could see him more clearly.

Mr. Frisbee examined Caesar for a minute or two in silence.

"Where did you find it?" he asked. "How did it come into your possession?"

"Someone left it in our yard," Jupe told him, deciding to keep Blinky out of it.

"Who?"

"We don't know," Pete said. "We just found him there. That's why we came to you. We thought you might know . . ."

Mr. Frisbee shook his head. He chuckled.

"That's not a Belgian Racing Homer," he said. "Or rather, it is and it isn't. You see, that's a hen pigeon, a female, and they don't race hens."

"Oh, but—" Bob seemed about to say something, then changed his mind. He closed his mouth with a snap.

"Then you wouldn't have any idea who he, I mean she, might belong to?" Jupe asked.

"No idea in the world." Mr. Frisbee shrugged again. Jupe thought he was smiling. It was difficult to tell through all that beard. "Sorry I couldn't help you boys. And please give my best regards to Miss Melody."

Jupe said they would and thanked Mr. Frisbee for his time. The Three Investigators trooped back onto Main Street with Caesar.

They had to wait to wheel their bicycles off the sidewalk while a black car pulled away from the curb and swept past them.

Jupe and Pete started to mount up. Bob stopped them, motioning them out of sight of the jewelry store.

"What is it?" Jupe asked him.

"I'm not sure." Bob took off his glasses and polished them, frowning. "But either Parker Frisbee doesn't know anything about racing pigeons—I mean absolutely nothing—or else he was lying to us."

"Why would he lie?" Pete prompted him.

"I don't know." Bob put his glasses back on. "But that book I got from the library this morning said they do race hens, female pigeons. Some of the world's champions have been hens."

Jupe looked at him, then at his watch. "It's close to dinner time," he said. "I vote we all go home, then meet after dinner at Headquarters to review the whole case."

"Okay," Pete agreed. "But if we're going to keep Caesar, or Caesaress, if she really is a she, I vote we move that big cage into Headquarters, so he or she can have a safe place to live. Okay?"

"Okay." Jupe nodded, getting onto his bicycle.

It was the first thing they did when they met after dinner. The chicken-wire cage was too big to get through the tunnel entrance to the office, but the Three Investigators had other secret ways of entering Headquarters. One of them, known as Emergency One, was down a rope through the skylight in the roof of the mobile home.

Pete went first, clambering over the junk that was piled high against the trailer. As soon as he had climbed down the rope, Jupe and Bob lowered Caesar in his small cage. Then they managed to squeeze the pigeon's new, larger home through the skylight and lower that too. Bob followed.

Jupe was the last one down the rope, pulling the skylight closed behind him. Pete and Bob were already moving Caesar from the small cage to the bigger one. Jupe scarcely glanced at them. His eyes went immediately to the answering machine connected to the phone.

Jupe's eyes gleamed almost as brightly as Mr. Frisbee's. The light was on. There was a message on the tape for them. Blinky, Jupe thought. He did call. So it *was* the man in the green van. . . . Jupe's mind was racing as he hurried to the answering machine.

"Listen to this," he said, switching on the tape and the loudspeaker attached to it.

Bob and Pete paused, listening. Jupe sat down in his swivel chair so he could give his full attention to the message.

"Help!" a woman's voice said. "I need your help! Oh, please, do help me!" Maureen Melody was almost singing in her agitation.

"There's a murderer at large! I went out just now and found his poor dead body . . . " Her voice faltered as she choked back a sob.

"Edgar Allan Poe," she managed to wail. "He's been beaten to death! And then I found another corpse. One of my beautiful hawks. Oh, help me. Please help me. Somebody's murdering my birds!"

5
Danger in the Woods

"When I found your card and saw that you were detectives," Maureen Melody said, "why, it seemed like a message from destiny."

The Three Investigators had biked back to her house and were sitting with her in the soundproof room.

"You see, I didn't want to call the police," she went on, reaching up to stroke the parrot on her shoulder. "I've had so much trouble with them already. Always coming up here and saying my neighbors are complaining about my darling birds. What could they possibly have to complain about?"

Maybe your neighbors are the unfriendly type who like a little quiet now and then, Pete thought.

He didn't say anything.

The First Investigator was busy examining the bodies of the two dead birds that were lying on a white cloth on the table. The magpie's head had been crushed in, as though by a blow from a stick, but there were no marks of violence on the hawk. Perhaps it had been poisoned, Jupe thought.

"What do you feed your hawks?" he asked Miss Melody.

"Why, meat, of course," she told him. "Hawks are carnivorous, you know. And then, they're such clever hunters. They feed themselves too. They hunt mice and rats and rabbits and . . ." She gestured vaguely with her plump white hand. "And whatever comes their way. I'm afraid they're rather naughty sometimes."

"Cruel," the parrot on her shoulder screeched. "Cruel. Cruel."

Jupe nodded. "Where did you find these bodies?" he asked.

"Edgar Allan Poe was on the edge of the lawn. And when I picked him up, the poor darling, I saw . . ."

She took a small lace handkerchief from her pocket and pressed it against her mouth, too overcome by the memory to go on.

"My beautiful hawk was on the ground among the trees," she managed to gasp out at last. "Where I usually leave the food for them. But he wasn't eating. He was just lying there . . . so still."

Jupe shook his head sympathetically.

"Could we see the place?" he suggested.

"Of course." Maureen Melody glanced at the French windows. It was almost dark outside. "I'll get a flashlight," she said.

"It's okay," Jupe told her. "We've got our own bicycle headlights. If you'll just show us the place, then we'll go on from there and make a thorough search."

The birds had grown quiet now that the sun had set. As the Three Investigators followed Miss Melody across the lawn with their bicycle headlights, they could hear only the occasional hoot of an owl, the mocking laughter of a cockatoo from the darkness of the trees.

"Edgar Allan Poe was just there," Maureen Melody told them brokenly, stopping and pointing at the ground.

Jupe shone his light at the spot she had indicated. He stooped and picked up a bloodstained feather. Miss Melody shivered.

"And the hawk was over there." She pointed again. "And now, if you don't mind, I think . . . I think I'll leave you and go and lie down."

She crossed her arms in front of her as though hugging herself and hurried toward the house.

Jupe wasn't sorry to see her go. He felt a real sympathy for Maureen Melody, but her grieving made it difficult for him to concentrate on the job at hand.

He walked over to where the dead hawk had been found. There were no feathers there. No shreds of meat. If the hawk had been poisoned, it had either finished its meal before dying or, possibly, Jupe thought, whoever had poisoned it had returned and cleared away the leftovers.

He shone his light carefully in a wide circle over the ground.

"Too bad," he said thoughtfully.

"What's too bad?" Bob wondered what was going on in the First Investigator's mind.

"Stony ground."

Jupe didn't feel like explaining himself any more thoroughly than that. There was work to do.

"Right," he said. "Let's split up. Bob, you take that side of the woods. And Pete, you take that side. And I'll take the middle. Okay?"

"Okay," Pete agreed. "But just tell me one thing first, will you, Jupe?"

"What?"

"What are we looking for?"

"Footprints." Jupe shone his light on the ground again. "He didn't leave any here because it's too stony. But it rained a couple of days ago and there should be quite a lot of soft soil among the trees. From what Miss Melody said about her neighbors, I don't think she has many human visitors, so if we do find a man's footprints, they're likely to be, well, the murderer's."

"Great," Pete told him. "So we find the

murderer's footprints. What do we do then? Take a plaster cast of them and try to find out where he bought his shoes?"

Jupe sighed.

"Blinky," he explained patiently. "Didn't you notice his shoes? They were rather large and had unusually pointed toes. Do you understand now?"

"Sure," Bob said. "If we find some pointed footprints then they're probably Blinky's. And if they're not pointed, well, that tells us something too."

"It tells us they're *not* Blinky's," Pete said, nodding. "What'll we do if we find something?"

"Signal with your bicycle light," Jupe told him. "Three longs and three shorts, until you get an answering flash."

The Investigators split up and set off into the woods.

Jupiter crouched slightly as he walked forward step by step, shining his light on the ground in a wide arc in front of him. Unfortunately, in choosing the middle section of the woods he seemed to have picked the most umpromising part. He was in an area of thick bushes and narrow gravel paths. There was very little soft soil and no sign of any footprints.

He was wondering if the others were having any better luck when he suddenly stopped moving. The beam of his light had picked out something dark in the bushes to his right.

He stared at it for a moment, then bent almost double and moved eagerly toward it. He went down on his knees, bringing his light closer to it.

Suddenly, from somewhere in the darkness, a screech owl called. The bird's cry didn't exactly distract Jupiter's attention, but it kept him from hearing the furtive movement behind him.

The first thing he did hear was a soft whistling sound. Instinctively, he moved quickly away from it. As the heavy stick came down it just missed his head, whistling past his ear and striking him hard on the shoulder.

For a second Jupe's whole right arm was deadened with the pain. He had just enough strength left in his fingers not to drop the bicycle light. He rolled over onto his back, clutching the light against his chest.

As he moved, the beam of light from the bicycle headlight swept upward. It traveled over a black slicker and held on a man's face.

Or what could be seen of the man's face. And that was very little. Only his nose and the dark glasses he was wearing showed like clearings in the forest of dark hair that covered his chin, his upper lip, and most of both cheeks.

For a moment the man seemed paralyzed by the light. Then he turned and plunged away into the bushes.

Jupe didn't try to go after him. He stumbled to his feet, rubbing his shoulder until some of the pain left his arm. When a little of the numbness had gone out of it, he aimed his bicycle light to one side, covering and uncovering the beam with one hand, flashing out the arranged call signal. Three longs and three shorts. He went on doing that until he saw Pete's answering flashes through the trees.

"Jupe?"

"Here," he called back.

Pete made his way to him out of the bushes. A moment later Bob joined them from his section of the woods. Jupe began to rub his shoulder again. He was still in some pain and he couldn't hide it from his friends.

"What happened?" Bob asked anxiously.

"Parker Frisbee," Jupe told him. "He attacked me with a stick. Luckily I managed to shine the light on his face and that seemed to scare him off. He ran away, over in that direction." Jupe pointed with his aching arm.

"You didn't see or hear him, did you, Bob?"

Bob shook his head. "There were so many bushes," he explained, "that I hadn't gotten very far. If he was making for the gates he wouldn't have passed anywhere near me."

"Do you think we ought to go after him?" Pete asked cautiously. The idea of chasing a man armed with a stick among the dark trees didn't appeal to him in the least.

"No." The idea didn't appeal to Jupe either.

Besides, he had unfinished business where he was. "I found something," he said.

He turned and shone his bike light into the bushes until its beam picked out what he had seen before he was attacked. He knelt down again, examining it. Bob and Pete knelt beside him.

"Holy crow," Pete said softly. "It looks like a—"

"Yes," Jupe agreed. "That's exactly what it is. A dead pigeon."

It was a very dead pigeon. Most of its head and body had been savagely torn away. There was very little left of it except its bloodstained tail feathers, part of one wing, and its legs.

Jupe reached forward and lifted one of its feet. Fastened around its ankle was a thin aluminum band. Jupe unfastened it, holding it close to Bob's light. The strip of aluminum had been folded over as though to conceal something inside it. Jupe carefully straightened the metal and took out a folded slip of paper.

It was a thin white strip about the size of a message in a Chinese fortune cookie. And like the message in a fortune cookie there was something written on it.

The Three Investigators craned closer trying to read what it was.

"Beats me," Pete said.

Jupe had to admit that it puzzled him too. He couldn't even make out what the handwritten letters were. They weren't like the letters in the English alphabet. He didn't think they were Greek letters either. They looked more like . . .

"Chinese," Bob suggested. "Or Japanese, I bet. It reminds me of the writing in the Japanese books and newspapers at the library. There are a lot of Japanese readers in town, and I'm always putting Japanese books back on the shelves."

Jupe nodded thoughtfully and put the slip away in his shirt pocket. He leaned forward, examining the dead pigeon again.

"Look," he said excitedly. "Look at its left foot."

Bob and Pete looked.

Although the pigeon's feet and legs didn't seem to have been damaged by whoever had killed it, there were only two toes on its left foot.

6
A Furtive Feast

"I can't tell you how grateful I am to you," Hector Sebastian said. "It isn't often I get a chance to fix my own lunch."

It was the morning after the discovery of the dead pigeon. Hector Sebastian and the Three Investigators were gathered in the kitchen of his home in the hills near Malibu.

The house had once been a restaurant called Charlie's Place. Sebastian had bought it after his mystery novel, *Dark Legacy,* was sold to the movies, and he was gradually converting it into what he called a stately home.

There had been no need to convert the kitchen. It was a large, light room, magnificently equipped with stoves, steam tables, freezers, refrigerators, griddles, everything needed to prepare meals for fifty or sixty people.

It was the kind of kitchen that would make any ordinary chef roll up his sleeves and plan delicious five-course dinners.

Unfortunately Hoang Van Don, Hector Sebastian's Vietnamese houseman, was no ordinary chef. There had been a time when Don had taken his menus from late-night TV commercials. Frozen pizzas, fish fingers, and canned spaghetti dishes had appeared with monotonous regularity on Sebastian's table.

The mystery writer remembered those days now with surprising nostalgia. Some months ago Don had discovered daytime television. He had become devoted to a series of health food gurus who recommended such delicacies as cold mashed turnips and raw fish.

At the moment Don was out of the house, doing a favor for the Three Investigators.

"Bacon and eggs and sausages and ham and, while we're at it, french fried potatoes?" Hector suggested to his three young friends, lifting the things out of the grocery bag he had had delivered from the local store.

It sounded good to Pete. He remembered one lunch in the writer's home that had consisted of nothing but boiled brown rice.

"What's Don into these days?" Pete asked. "Is he still giving you raw fish, Mr. Sebastian?"

"I wish he were." Hector Sebastian was busy chopping up the potatoes for french fries. "Last night, for dinner, I had seaweed."

Pete scooped the potatoes into a wire net and lowered them into the already heated oil. Bob spread the ham and sausages onto the sizzling griddle, and Sebastian limped over to the sideboard for the eggs.

Sebastian had once been a private detective in New York. He had started writing mystery novels while he was recovering from a serious leg injury, and he still needed a cane to get around.

"Thank heaven Don's friend lives so far away," Sebastian said as he and the three boys settled down to their meal around the kitchen table.

Don was off seeing a Japanese friend from his karate class at a Malibu health club. The houseman had agreed to ask his friend to translate the message the boys had found the night before.

"Don won't be back for at least another hour," Sebastian continued. "We'll have time to clear everything away before he returns." He smiled at the First Investigator across the table. "No french fries for you, Jupe?"

Jupiter shook his head politely. He was feeling pleasantly virtuous about not helping himself to the potatoes and was thoroughly enjoying his lunch. After all, ham and eggs, even sausages, weren't really that fattening.

"Now what's all this about secret messages in Japanese?" Hector Sebastian asked him. "Or perhaps you feel it's too early to tell me about this latest case of yours."

The First Investigator hesitated. He knew what a lively interest the mystery writer took in all their cases, and he was more than grateful for the friendly help Hector Sebastian had given them in the past. The trouble was that he was still far from sure what the mystery of the murdered birds *was* all about.

He explained how they had found the message attached to a dead pigeon's ankle, how Bob had guessed and then confirmed at the library that the message was written in Japanese.

"Well, I'm very glad you thought of coming to me with it," Sebastian told him. "Or rather to Don. I haven't had such a good lunch in months."

He reached for the cane hanging on the back of his chair and pushed himself to his feet.

"And now I think we'd better destroy the evidence of our feast before he gets back," he said. "I'll never hear the last of it if Don finds out I've been eating real food."

The three boys had wiped off the griddle and were putting the last clean plates back on the shelves when they heard the Vietnamese houseman's car turn into the driveway.

"Quick. Into the other room," Hector Sebastian warned them, limping ahead of them into the huge living room with its row of windows overlooking the ocean. He sat down at the patio table at the end of the room. The Three Investigators joined him there.

Jupe heard the back door into the kitchen open and close as Don entered the house. He sat up tensely in his chair. In a second now he would know what that message from the dead pigeon's leg said. He would be one step closer to understanding, and he hoped solving, the mystery of the murdered birds.

He waited, his neck tingling with excitement.

He heard the Vietnamese houseman's footsteps cross the kitchen. He heard them pause there. He heard what sounded like a sniff.

It was almost a minute before Hoang Van Don finally appeared around the bookshelves that separated Sebastian's study from the living room.

"Well?" Jupe was on his feet. "What does the message say?"

The Vietnamese halted a few feet from the table. He stood there with his hands on his hips.

"First I have question," he said. "Question about what—"

"Please," Jupe pleaded with him. "Please. The message. What did it say?"

Don hesitated, frowning. He seemed to be coming to a decision.

"Okay," he said at last. "I answer your question first. Then you answer mine."

He took a scrap of paper from his pocket and glanced at it.

"Message says, 'No pearls today.' "

"No pearls today," Jupe repeated thoughtfully. His mind was racing. Pearls. Pigeons. Dead hawks. Magpies. Parker Frisbee.

"And now you answer my question," the Vietnamese said sternly. "What is that horrible, disgusting smell in kitchen?"

7
The Showdown

When they left Hector Sebastian's house, the Three Investigators made straight for Head-quarters.

There were so many unanswered questions puzzling Jupiter that he couldn't wait to sit down in his swivel chair behind his desk and thrash them out aloud with Bob and Pete. What this case needed was a real think session, he felt.

The three boys wheeled their bicycles into the junkyard and headed for the hidden mobile home.

"So there you are." Jupe's Aunt Mathilda came out of the office cabin and stood facing them.

She was a kindly woman and she had been happy to make a home for Jupe when his parents died. But Aunt Mathilda had one small weakness.

She loved to see boys working.

She had work for them to do now. A load of angle irons that Uncle Titus had bought had to be sorted and put away in wooden boxes.

Jupe sighed, looking at the great metal pile. He knew there was no escape once Aunt Mathilda had made up her mind. The job would take them at least two hours, he figured.

It took them a little longer than that because when they thought they were finished, Aunt Mathilda insisted on inspecting every box of angle irons before she would let the boys go.

"All right," she said at last. "You've done a good job. You can go back to your puzzles now."

Jupiter had never explained to his aunt that he and Bob and Pete were serious investigators. Aunt Mathilda thought they were members of a club that met to solve riddles they found in newspapers and magazines.

He waited until she had gone back into the junkyard office, then led the way to his outdoor workshop. There he lifted aside the iron grating that just seemed to be leaning against an old printing press.

Beyond it was the entrance to the secret tunnel to Headquarters—a large corrugated pipe known as Tunnel Two. The three boys crawled into the pipe, Pete going last so he could pull the grating back into place after him.

When he reached the end of the tunnel, Jupe

pushed up the trap door above his head and climbed out into the office at Headquarters.

He glanced at once at the answering machine beside the phone. No light. No messages. He sat down behind his desk. Pete sprawled in an old rocking chair with his feet up on a drawer of the filing cabinet. Bob sat on a stool, leaning back against the wall, and took out his notebook.

It was Jupe as usual who opened the think session.

"Pearls," he said. "They keep cropping up in this case."

"So do pigeons," Pete pointed out, watching Caesar hopping about in his chicken-wire cage. "Two-toed pigeons. Three-toed pigeons. Live pigeons. Dead pigeons."

"Pearls," Jupe repeated firmly. "That message said, 'No pearls today.' Maureen Melody has a passion for pearls. She had a magpie that used to bring her pearls."

"Edgar Allan Poe." Bob nodded, looking up from his notebook. "He came hopping into the room with a pearl in his beak when we were there. And Miss Melody said, 'That's the third pearl he's brought me this month.' "

"Then somebody killed Edgar Allan Poe," Jupe continued thoughtfully. "Probably Parker Frisbee. And Frisbee's a jeweler who buys and sells pearls. So if pearls are the fundamental issue in this mystery . . ." Jupe sometimes lapsed into rather elaborate language when he was thinking aloud. "If pearls are the prime motivation, the question is where do the pigeons come in? What's the connection?"

He broke off. The phone was ringing. Jupe switched on the loudspeaker so that the other two Investigators could hear what the caller said. Then he picked up the receiver.

"Hello. The Three Investigators here," he said.

"Hello. Is that Jupiter Jones?" There was a familiar note of anxiety in the man's voice. "I want to speak to Jupiter Jones."

"Jupiter Jones speaking," Jupe assured him.

"Oh." There was a pause. "I hope you'll remember me. We met at the Seahorse Diner a couple of days ago. I left a package behind. I mean, I forgot it. And when I went back for it, the waitress told me she thought you'd taken it with you when you left."

Jupe covered the mouthpiece with his hand.

"Blinky," he whispered excitedly to the other two Investigators.

"Hello?" The man sounded even more nervous. "Hello? Are you there?"

"Yes, I'm here," Jupe told him. "And certainly, I remember the whole occasion very clearly."

There was another, longer pause.

"Have you got it?" the man asked at last. "Have you got my package?"

"Yes, we have," Jupe answered. "A large square

box, covered with cheesecloth. It's quite safe. We've been keeping it for you, hoping you'd call."

"Oh." The man sounded relieved. "That's very kind of you. I mean, I think you boys deserve a reward. If you'll bring the box back to me, I-I'll pay you twenty dollars for your trouble."

"Thank you," Jupe told him. "Where would you like us to bring it?"

"Well, I know where you live—I mean, I know you live in Rocky Beach, so why don't I meet you somewhere around there? Say, in the parking lot of the Trustee Bank."

"That would be fine," Jupe agreed. "What time would suit you?"

"Nine o'clock tonight?"

Jupe agreed to that too.

"Nine o'clock," the man repeated in a nervous way.

"Wow," Pete said as Jupe hung up the phone. "Twenty dollars."

The First Investigator didn't seem to have heard him. He was pinching his lower lip, deep in thought.

"I kept that cheesecloth." Bob opened the filing cabinet. "Do you want to put Caesar in the smaller cage and the cloth back the way it was?"

Jupe didn't answer for a minute, then he shook his head.

"First let's examine what Blinky said." Jupiter was thinking aloud again. "He said, 'I know where you live.' Then he corrected himself and said, 'I mean, I know you live in Rocky Beach.' And he would know that from the telephone exchange on our card. But I think he was telling the truth the first time. He does know exactly where I live."

"So Blinky was the one who switched the pigeons that first night," Bob put in.

"Precisely," Jupe agreed. "That's my hunch anyway. So Blinky knew I was lying when I tried to make him think we hadn't opened the package. He knew I was bluffing and he didn't call my bluff. And if we take the package back to him the way it was, he'll say, thank you very much—"

"And give us twenty dollars," Pete reminded him.

"And walk off with Caesar, pretending he thinks it's his two-toed pigeon under the cheesecloth. Then we'll never hear from him again. And there goes our best lead in the whole case."

"So what do you want to do?" Bob asked.

"Have a showdown," Jupe told him. "Confront him with Caesar in his unwrapped cage. Then maybe we can make Blinky answer some questions. What do you think, Pete?"

Pete scratched his head. "Okay," he agreed cautiously. "I'd hate to lose that twenty bucks. But I guess you're right. If we're ever going to solve this case, we need some answers from Blinky."

Bob and Pete had to go back to their own homes for supper. Before they left, the Three Investigators arranged to meet in the parking lot of the Trustee Bank at ten to nine that night.

At half past eight Jupe strapped the smaller cage with Caesar inside it to the carrier of his bicycle and pedaled into town.

The bank was on Main Street not far from Frisbee's jewelry store. Jupe wheeled his bicycle into the parking lot behind the big white building. Few cars used the lot after the bank closed, and the wide space, surrounded on three sides by closed office buildings, was in half-darkness.

Jupe leaned his bicycle against the wall of the bank, turned off the light, and unstrapped the cage from the carrier.

He looked around. There were only half a dozen cars scattered around the darkened lot and there was no sign of life in any of them.

Jupe glanced at his watch. A quarter to nine. Fifteen minutes before the arranged meeting with Blinky. Five minutes before Bob and Pete were due to arrive. Jupe decided to wait for his friends at the entrance to the lot where there was more light from the street lamps. He started toward it.

"Stop right where you are, boy."

The voice came out of the shadows behind him.

Jupe did as he was told. He stopped right where he was, holding the cage against his chest.

"Now turn around slowly."

Jupe turned around. Just as slowly as he could.

The figure of a man moved toward him out of the gloom. The man was holding his right hand out in front of him. He was gripping something in it. Something that gleamed slightly, even in the half darkness.

To Jupe the gleaming thing looked horribly like the nickel-plated barrel of a gun. He couldn't take his eyes off it.

"Now put that cage down in front of you."

Jupe leaned forward and put it down. The man moved a little closer. Still pointing the gun at Jupe, he crouched over the cage and took a good look at it. Making sure, Jupe guessed, that the pigeon was inside it.

"Good."

The man straightened. For a moment then Jupe could see him quite clearly. He could see the shiny black slicker the man was wearing. He could see the man's dark glasses, the heavy growth of black beard that covered most of his face. Parker Frisbee!

"Now turn around and lie down on the ground."

For the first time it struck Jupe that the man's voice was curiously low-pitched and carefully controlled. It sounded as though he were speaking with great effort. He's almost as scared as I am and he's trying to hide it, was the thought that flashed through Jupe's mind.

The man shifted the gun slightly in a

threatening way. Jupe turned around and lay down on the ground.

"Put your hands behind you."

As Jupe obeyed, he heard a tearing sound. Like someone ripping a piece of cloth, he thought. Or . . . or pulling a length of adhesive tape off a roll, he realized more accurately a moment later as his wrists were firmly taped together behind his back.

He didn't try to struggle. The memory of the gleaming barrel of that gun was too vivid in his mind. He lay quite still while his ankles were firmly taped together too.

He continued to lie motionless as he heard the man's footsteps move away from him. The lights of a car went on somewhere behind him. Bound hand and foot, he could not really raise his head, but he managed to turn it slightly, and very cautiously. He peered around toward the light.

The car was already in motion. The approaching darkness made it impossible to identify the car. It roared past him some twenty yards from where he lay, did a screeching turn toward the exit to the parking lot, and vanished into the street.

Jupe lay there blaming himself. He should have had the sense to wait for Pete and Bob, he thought. He shouldn't have walked blindly into the half-darkness of the parking lot. He should have left his bicycle . . .

He heard footsteps approaching from the entrance to the lot. He saw the flash of a bicycle light.

"Pete," he called. "Bob."

A moment later his two friends were bending over him, gently peeling the tape from his wrists and ankles. Jupe rolled over and sat up. The skin of his wrists was sore from the peeled-off tape. He rubbed them as he explained to the other two Investigators what had happened.

Pete whistled softly. "He had a gun?"

"To the best of my knowledge that's precisely what he had." Jupe climbed to his feet. "Of course, I didn't ask him to fire it, so I can't be sure it was loaded." He brushed off the knees of his pants. "Did you see anything?" he asked.

"A car." Bob nodded. "A black car." He frowned, taking off his glasses and polishing them on his sleeve. "And that's funny because I thought it was Blinky's. I noticed the letters on the license plate and they were MOK. Like—"

"Like the black car Blinky drove off in from the Seahorse Diner," Jupe finished for him. "And like . . ."

He didn't complete the sentence because he couldn't be absolutely sure. But he remembered the black car that had swept past them when they were coming out of Parker Frisbee's jewelry store. He had only glimpsed it for an instant and he hadn't had time to read all three letters on the plate, but he was sure the first one of them had been an M.

"So what do we do now?" Pete asked. "Frisbee's got Caesar and . . ."

"And when Blinky shows up what are we going to tell him?" Bob asked.

Jupe looked at his watch. It was two minutes to nine. He still felt a little shaken by the memory of that gun.

"We're not going to tell him anything," he decided hastily. "Because we're not going to wait for him. We're going to ramble and scramble and we'll meet at Headquarters in the morning."

"Ramble and scramble" was the signal the Three Investigators used when in a tight spot. It meant to split up and head off in different directions. Now all three jumped on their bicycles and pedaled off to their own homes.

Jupe slept badly that night. There was too much on his mind. As Pete had said, they had lost Caesar. And there had been no showdown with Blinky. There was no information to report to Maureen Melody either. They couldn't very well go to her and tell her they thought her friend Parker Frisbee had been killing her birds. They couldn't prove it anyway. And, worse than that, Jupe couldn't think of any reasonable explanation for *why* Frisbee had murdered Edgar Allan Poe. If he really had, that is.

The case seemed to be going badly for The Three Investigators. The only hope now appeared to be that Blinky would call again to ask why they hadn't kept their appointment.

At least that would give them a chance to talk to Blinky. When Blinky heard that Caesar had been kidnapped, he might tell them something that would give them another lead.

Maybe they should have waited for him in the parking lot after all, was Jupe's last regretful thought as he finally fell asleep.

Since the beginning of summer vacation, Jupiter had been eating a very light breakfast. Dry toast and skimmed milk. His aunt Mathilda was worried about his recent, unusual loss of appetite. When she urged Jupiter the next morning to have ham and eggs, "And some nice hash browns, too," the First Investigator was too low in spirits to refuse her. He ate everything she put in front of him before going out to the junkyard to wait for his friends.

He was just approaching the workshop and the Tunnel Two entrance to Headquarters when he saw it. It saw him too and strutted eagerly to meet him.

Jupe bent down and the pigeon let him pick it up in his hands. He stared at it, examining every feather of its gleaming wings and tail. He looked at its sleek, gray head and alert eyes.

There was no question about it. He would know this particular pigeon anywhere. He couldn't be mistaken.

It was Caesar.

8
Visitors from the East

"It's Caesar, all right," Pete said. "I'd swear to it. Those markings on his tail feathers. Besides, it's obvious he recognizes us. Don't you, Caesar?"

The Three Investigators were gathered in the office at Headquarters. Caesar, back in his big cage, was hopping cheerfully about, pecking at his corn.

"Parker Frisbee steals him from me at gunpoint." The First Investigator was pinching his lip so hard he had pulled it halfway down to his chin. "And then a few hours later he brings him back and lets him loose in our yard. Why? Why? Why?" It seemed to Jupe that there were more "Whys?" in this case than in any he had ever encountered.

"Maybe he didn't bring him back." Bob's glasses had slipped down his nose. He pushed them up into place.

"What do you mean?" Pete asked him. "Caesar's here, isn't he?"

"That book about pigeons," Bob explained. "During the Second World War they used homing pigeons to carry messages. If the army was advancing, they had to keep moving the pigeon coops. And they found that a really highly trained homer would get used to a different base in two or three days . . ."

"So it would fly back to its new home instead of the old one." Jupe nodded encouragingly. "I think you've got something, Bob. Maybe Caesar doesn't belong to Parker Frisbee and he wanted to return him to his real owner." He frowned. "Don't ask me why. But if that was what he was trying to do, the simplest thing would be to just turn him loose and let him fly home."

"This is your home now, isn't it, Caesar?" Pete put his finger through the chicken wire and stroked the pigeon's sleek head. "So you came back here, and I'm very glad—"

He broke off at the sound of a voice over the loudspeaker.

"Jupe. Jupe."

It was Aunt Mathilda. Jupe had rigged up a microphone in the yard so he could hear his aunt calling him when he was in Headquarters.

"Jupe. Bob. Pete. Where are you?"

Jupiter sighed. A summons from Aunt Mathilda usually meant one thing—work. She had a job for them to do. He hoped it wasn't another load of angle irons. Maybe she just needed help with the Saturday crowd of customers.

The Three Investigators left their carefully concealed Headquarters by the exit known as Door Four, which brought them out into the back of the yard. Walking around a pile of lumber, they approached Aunt Mathilda from behind.

She jumped when Jupiter tapped her on the shoulder. "So there you are," she said. "I never know where you boys have squirreled yourselves away."

Jupe did his best to look cooperative. "What's the job?" he asked.

But for once Aunt Mathilda had not called the boys to put them to work. There were two men asking for them, she said. They were out by the gate.

The two men were standing beside a green van that was parked in the road. They were about thirty years old, short and wiry, and they were both wearing T-shirts and faded blue jeans. They were both Japanese.

"You are Jupe, Pete, and Bob?" one of them asked, stepping forward.

Jupe said they were.

"You know Hoang Van Don?"

"Yes, we do," Jupe told him.

The man turned to his companion and said something in a language Jupe guessed must be Japanese. The second man nodded and answered in the same language.

"My friend here is named Kyoto. He would be very pleased if you would let him ask you some questions," the first man explained. "Except unfortunately Kyoto does not speak English. So I will interpret for him. Okay?"

Jupe said that would be fine.

"First question. You gave Hoang Van Don a message written in Japanese. You asked him to take it to a Japanese friend to have it translated. Don's friend told Kyoto about it because he recognized Kyoto's handwriting."

That didn't sound like a question to Jupe. He waited.

"Where did you find the message?"

Jupe thought that over for a second. He didn't have to answer, but he figured that if he did, maybe Kyoto might be willing to answer some questions in return.

"On a dead pigeon," Jupe said. "The message was fastened around its leg."

The interpreter smiled politely. He walked over to Kyoto, and taking him by the arm, led him away to the front of the van.

Bob watched the two Japanese standing there,

talking together in their own language. It struck him how alike they looked. They both had the same straight black hair, the same rather high cheekbones, the same pale brown skin. He wasn't sure, if he saw one of them on the street, that he would know whether it was Kyoto or the interpreter.

Or maybe that was just because they were both Japanese, he thought. They probably didn't look in the least alike to each other. And maybe they felt the same way about him and Pete and Jupe. Maybe to them a lot of Caucasians looked alike. Jupe studied the two men as they stood by the van, searching for some small differences in their looks.

"The green van," Jupe suddenly whispered to Bob. "It's the same van that Blinky followed from the Seahorse Diner. If we could follow it . . ."

Jupe glanced at the two Japanese. They were still busy talking.

"The beeper," Jupe whispered urgently. "Do you think you could get it?"

"I'll try," Bob whispered back.

He moved slightly away from Jupe. "I think Aunt Mathilda's calling," he said loudly so the interpreter could hear him. "I'd better see what she wants."

He turned and walked back through the gate and hurried to Headquarters.

"Second question." The interpreter and Kyoto

walked back to Jupe again. "Where did you find the dead pigeon?"

The First Investigator thought that over for a second too. Although he was a naturally truthful boy, there were times when investigators had to stretch the truth a little. Particularly when they were protecting a client. And in the case of the murdered birds it was Maureen Melody who had called him and asked for help. The way Jupe looked at it, that made Miss Melody their client. It was his job to protect her.

"We found the dead pigeon on the road," he said.

"What road?"

"On the other side of town." At least that was close to the truth.

The interpreter smiled politely again. "Third question," he said. "How do you think the pigeon died?"

"I don't know." That was the absolute truth. Jupe wished he knew the answer himself.

"What did the body look like? You think somebody shot it?"

"No." Jupe shook his head. "It didn't look as if it had been shot." He could hear Bob coming back, crossing the salvage yard behind him. "I suppose it could have been hit by a car," he suggested helpfully.

"Good. Thank you." Kyoto and the interpreter were moving toward the front door of the van.

Bob was just coming through the gate. Jupe reached out and touched the interpreter's arm.

"Excuse me," he said. "Would you mind if I asked you a question now?"

It was the interpreter's turn to think things over for a second. "Okay," he agreed.

"The message said, 'No pearls today.' At least that's what Don's Japanese friend said."

"Yes."

Bob was back, standing beside Jupe. Glancing down, Jupe could barely see a small metal object clasped in Bob's hands. The beeper.

"Well, what does that mean?" Jupe asked. "No pearls today." He was a good actor when he felt like it, and one of his best roles was playing dumb. "It just doesn't seem to make any sense," he said, dropping his jaw a little and making his face as vacant as an empty box. "What pearls? And why aren't there any today?"

He nudged Bob slightly and moved away from him to the front of the van. The interpreter and Kyoto walked along with Jupe. "I'd be awfully grateful if you could explain it to me," Jupe told the interpreter.

The interpreter smiled his polite smile.

"It's very simple," he said. "My friend Kyoto is a gardener. He has a vegetable farm up the coast. He sells his vegetables in a Japanese market and the market man needs to know what he has to sell . . ."

Jupe listened with the same vacant stare. He was watching Bob as he edged around to the back of the van. He saw Bob bend down and quickly reach under the rear bumper.

"So Kyoto sends messages to the market man by carrier pigeon," the interpreter was saying. "He tells him 'lots of carrots today.' Or, 'lots of celery.' Then the market man knows what he has to sell."

Jupe saw Bob straighten up and raise his right hand. He was no longer holding the small metal object in it.

"I see," the First Investigator said, using his most simpleminded voice. "And Kyoto raises pearls too?"

The interpreter laughed.

"Pearls are pearl onions," he explained. "No pearls today means no pearl onions."

"Oh. Thank you."

Jupe continued to look vacant as Kyoto and the interpreter climbed into the van and drove off. He stood still until it reached the bend in the street.

"Quick, Bob," he said. "The tracker."

Bob had left it just inside the gate. He brought it to Jupe, a small box with dials and a circular antenna on it. It looked like an old radio. It *had* been an old radio once. Jupe had converted it into a tracking device. He switched it on.

Beep-beep-beep.

The sound came out of the tracker at once. It

had picked up the signal from the electronic beeper that Bob had magnetically fastened under the back of the van.

Jupe swiveled the antenna, aiming south.

Beep-beep-beep. It was a little louder now.

"They're heading toward the coast," Jupe said. "Let's go after them."

Pete already had the three bicycles outside the gate. Jupe strapped the tracker to the handlebars of his bike. They mounted and rode off.

Jupe rode with one hand. With the other he could aim the antenna on the tracker to the left or right or straight ahead. By listening to the beeps grow louder or fainter, he could tell which way the van had turned.

The beeper's signal would reach them as long as they stayed within a mile of it. They could follow the van on their bicycles with no danger of being seen.

Jupe didn't think they'd have any trouble keeping up with it. He remembered how faltering the van's engine had sounded as it ground up the hill to the Seahorse Diner.

As he pedaled along, tracking the beeps with the antenna, the First Investigator just hoped the van wasn't going too far.

He didn't mind bicycling, and he knew the exercise was good for him—it would help work off that big breakfast this morning—but he did hope the van wasn't headed for San Francisco or anything like that.

Pearl onions, he thought. Kyoto and the interpreter must have thought he was really dumb if they expected him to believe that. But what were the Japanese going to such lengths to hide?

9

The Mysterious
Mr. Frisbee

After a few minutes of hard pedaling Jupe was
relieved to see that the green van couldn't be
heading for San Francisco or even Santa Monica.
It wasn't turning off onto the coast road. It was
going straight into town.

He could tell from the sound of the beeps and
the direction of the antenna on the tracking box
that the van was now moving down Main Street
in Rocky Beach. He signaled to Bob and Pete,
riding behind him, to go slowly. He didn't want to
catch up with the van if it had to stop for a red
light. Kyoto and his interpreter friend might see
the boys in their rearview mirror.

The Three Investigators passed Frisbee's
jewelry store and the Trustee Bank. *Beep-beep—*

And then suddenly the beeping stopped. Jupe held up his hand. The Three Investigators halted. Sitting astride his bicycle with his feet on the ground, Jupe turned the antenna so that it pointed to the left. No beep. He turned to the right this time. *Beep-beep-beep.* It was coming in loud and clear now.

Jupe gave a right-hand turn signal and led the way up the cross street that wound into the hills outside of town.

It was more difficult to track the van now because of the twists in the road. The beeps kept fading out altogether on the turns. But that didn't worry Jupe, even when there was no sound from the tracker for minutes at a time. He thought he knew where the van was going.

In the low hills on the northwest side of Rocky Beach were a few square blocks of neat frame houses set in their own tidy yards. The neighborhood was known as Little Tokyo because almost all the houses in it were owned or rented by Japanese.

Jupe held up his hand again as the boys entered Little Tokyo. The Three Investigators pulled to a stop. A hundred yards ahead of them, parked in the driveway of a one-story frame house, was the green van.

Jupe pulled his bicycle onto the sidewalk. Bob and Pete followed him. Standing among the trees that lined the street, they could keep an eye on the van without being seen from the house.

"Okay," Pete said. "So maybe that's where Kyoto lives and maybe it isn't. What do we do now?"

Jupe didn't answer. He was watching the van. He saw a man walk down the driveway past it. He must have come out of the house, Jupe decided. The man walked on to the street. There was a small red car parked there. He unlocked the car, got into it, and drove off.

"Was that Kyoto?" Bob wasn't sure. The two Japanese looked so much alike to him.

"No." Jupe shook his head. "That was the interpreter."

Bob didn't question that Jupe was right. But he couldn't help asking, "How did you know?"

"By everything," Jupe explained. "His walk, his eyes, his ears. Besides, didn't you notice the tooled belt he was wearing and that grease stain on his jeans?"

Bob hadn't. There were still times when the First Investigator's powers of observation astonished him.

"So now we can be almost sure that's Kyoto's house," Jupe went on. "But 'almost' isn't good enough. If only we could see if there's a name on the mailbox."

If there was, it was painted on the other side of the box. They would have to walk right past the house to find out.

"You'd better go alone, Bob," Jupe decided. "Pete's too tall and I'm too . . ." He hesitated, trying to find the right word. "I'm too stocky. If Kyoto happens to be looking out the window, he might recognize either of us. But if you take off your glasses and your Windbreaker, you'll probably look just like any other American kid to him. He won't remember ever having seen you before."

"Okay." Bob wasn't sure he was happy about being so ordinary-looking, but someone had to check the mailbox. So he put his glasses in his shirt pocket and unzipped the tan Windbreaker he was wearing. He walked toward the house with the green van parked in its driveway. He strolled on past the house, past the white mailbox at the bottom of the driveway, then casually paused and, pretending to pull up his socks, looked back.

J. KYOTO.

The name was painted in black letters on the box. Bob was preparing to saunter back to his friends when he thought he noticed something else. He couldn't be sure without his glasses, but it looked as though there had been another name on the box before Kyoto's.

He decided he had to make sure. Whatever the risk of being watched from Kyoto's house, he had to put his glasses back on. He pulled them out of his shirt pocket and slipped them on his nose.

He was right. The other name had been almost

covered up by a new coat of white paint, but he could still make out some of the old letters. How long ago had it been repainted? With a quick, cautious glance toward the house, Bob reached out and touched the mailbox. The black paint on the name was still wet. Then Kyoto had only just moved into the house.

Bob felt rather proud of himself, of his discovery and deduction. Jupe himself could hardly have done better. He couldn't wait to get back to his friends and report to them.

He had taken only two steps when he stopped as still as a statue. A man was coming down the driveway toward him. Seeing him, Bob felt as if he couldn't move. He felt petrified. There was no mistaking that short figure, that cutaway coat, those striped pants, that bushy black beard.

"Hey. Hey, you there."

Parker Frisbee had seen him. Bob wanted to run, but he didn't seem to be able to move his feet. It was like one of those nightmares when you lose all control of your legs. He stood there as Frisbee came closer and closer to him.

One good thing, Bob thought. At least he's not carrying a stick. Although he might have a gun in his pocket, of course.

"I'm glad I ran into you." Frisbee stopped a foot away from him. "I've been wanting to talk to you boys."

It was always difficult to tell whether the

jeweler was smiling or not because his beard was so thick. But Frisbee wasn't wearing his dark glasses and Bob could see that his eyes looked strangely cordial.

"Where are your friends?" Parker Frisbee asked.

Bob gestured vaguely toward the others. He was glad to discover that he had recovered the use of his limbs. He started to walk to where he had left Jupe and Pete. Frisbee walked beside him.

Bob was relieved to see that Jupe had spread Bob's Windbreaker over the handlebars of his bicycle, hiding the tracking box. He waited uneasily as Frisbee paused on the sidewalk and faced the other two Investigators.

"You boys often come up here to Little Tokyo?" he asked in a friendly way.

"There's a Japanese restaurant we sometimes go to," Jupe explained quickly. "Pete likes Japanese food."

"Oh, yes. The Fujiyama. It's very good. I sometimes go there myself. Well ..." Again Bob couldn't be sure if Frisbee was smiling or not. "Why don't you let me take you all to lunch there?"

For once even Jupe didn't know what to say.

The last time he had seen this man, Frisbee had been pointing a gun at the First Investigator while tying him up in the parking lot of the Trustee Bank. And the time before that he had been beating him with a stick. Now he was inviting them all to lunch as though none of that had ever happened.

"Oh, well, that's very kind of you," the First Investigator managed to mumble at last. "Thank you, Mr. Frisbee."

"Come on." Frisbee started briskly across the street. The Three Investigators followed him, wheeling their bicycles.

Bob edged his way close enough to Jupe to explain to him in a whisper what he had found out from Kyoto's mailbox. Jupe nodded without saying anything.

The boys chained their bicycles outside the restaurant and Parker Frisbee led them in to a big corner table. The waiter greeted the jeweler in Japanese. Frisbee answered him in the same language and ordered their food.

"I lived in Japan for a couple of years," he explained casually. "I was in the pearl business there. So I had to learn Japanese."

The waiter brought the tea and Frisbee poured for all of them.

"Now," he said, settling back in his chair. "I understand you boys have been doing a little private investigating."

This time Bob could see the jeweler was smiling. None of the Three Investigators said anything.

"For Miss Maureen Melody," Frisbee went on.

"Trying to find out who's been killing her birds."

Jupe nodded.

"And now my gardener, Kyoto, tells me you found a dead pigeon with a message on it."

Jupe nodded again.

"A message about the vegetables he was sending to the Japanese market."

"His pearl onions," Jupe agreed.

There was a long silence after that while the waiter spread a dozen little dishes on the table in front of them and they all began to eat.

"Did you find the dead pigeon in Miss Melody's garden?" Frisbee asked at last.

"No." Jupe's mouth was full of rice and salmon and bamboo shoots and a delicious salty sauce. He had to swallow before he could go on. "We found it in the road," he explained, deciding to keep to the same story he had told Kyoto.

Frisbee picked up his chopsticks and there was another long silence while they all went on eating.

"Well." The jeweler had finished. He wiped his mouth with a napkin and reached his hand into his inside pocket.

Pete froze, his fork halfway to his mouth. Frisbee wouldn't pull a gun on them here, would he, in a public restaurant? he thought desperately.

Frisbee pulled out his wallet.

"As you know, Miss Melody is a good friend of mine," he said, "as well as a valued customer." His eyes gleamed for an instant. "I know how upset she is about her dead birds, and I want to do everything I possibly can to help her." He opened his wallet and took something out of it.

It was a fifty-dollar bill. Frisbee handed it to Jupe.

"Here's a sort of retainer for you," he said. "To keep up your investigation for Miss Melody. And if you can find out who it is who's been killing those birds"—he slipped the wallet back in his pocket—"I'll be glad to give you another fifty dollars."

"Thank you." Jupe put the money away in his pocket. "We'll do the best we can, Mr. Frisbee," he promised.

"The best we can," he repeated outside on the sidewalk as the Three Investigators unchained their bicycles and watched Parker Frisbee stride briskly away down the street.

"You bet we will," Pete agreed. "For fifty dollars—" He checked himself, looking at Jupe.

The First Investigator was obviously lost in thought.

"We take Caesar into his shop to him," he said in his thinking-aloud voice. "If he wanted the pigeon all he had to do was say, yes, he recognized it, he knew who it belonged to, and thank you very much he would return it to its owner."

He shook his head as though he couldn't believe his own words. "Instead of that, he says, no, he's never seen Caesar before, and he lets us walk off with him. Then the next evening he kidnaps Caesar at gunpoint." He paused for a second, still shaking his head.

"He finds me in Miss Melody's woods and he attacks me with a stick," he went on. "Now he buys us lunch . . ."

He frowned unhappily for a moment as he thought about that. He had had a big breakfast today and now an enormous midday meal. Oh, well, this was no time to worry about his weight. There was too much else to think about.

"He buys us lunch," Jupe repeated. "He gives us fifty dollars and he promises us another fifty if we can find out who's killing Maureen Melody's birds. All that seems a little puzzling—I mean for the same man to do all those things. But there's something even more mysterious about Parker Frisbee . . ."

His voice trailed off.

"What?" Bob prompted him. "Go on. Tell us, Jupe. What's even more mysterious about him?"

"He only wears dark glasses at night."

10
The Pigeon Murderer Exposed

"What?" Pete shouted.

Jupe shook his head. "Never mind."

He knew it was hopeless to try to talk above the whistles and screeches and caws and chirpings that filled the woods on both sides of them.

It was late the next afternoon. The Three Investigators were wheeling their bicycles up Maureen Melody's drive.

After leaving Little Tokyo, Jupe had called Miss Melody and arranged to visit her the next morning. But just as the three boys were leaving the salvage yard for her house, Aunt Mathilda had stopped them and put them to work.

There had been rain during the night and she wanted the whole yard mopped out. Then all the old refrigerators and cooking stoves Uncle Titus had salvaged had to be wiped off. It had taken them many hours of valuable time that might have been spent trying to solve the mystery of Miss Melody's murdered birds.

Jupe shivered as he walked up to her house with his bicycle, remembering his awful experience in her woods. He hoped they would leave here well before dark.

Miss Melody answered the doorbell at once. She was wearing a black velvet dress with long sleeves, and as she led the three boys into the soundproof room she kept dabbing at her eyes with a small lace handkerchief.

"Look," she said, restraining a sob and pointing unsteadily at the table. The Three Investigators looked. Laid out on a white cloth was another dead hawk.

As Pete moved closer to the table, the parrot fluttered over from its perch and settled on his shoulder.

"It's so cruel." Miss Melody was openly sobbing now.

"Cruel," the parrot echoed her. "Cruel. Cruel."

Jupe was examining the dead bird. Its body showed no signs of violence. Like the other hawk it had probably been poisoned, he assumed.

"When did you find it, Miss Melody?" he asked.

Maureen Melody made an effort to control her grief. She dabbed at her eyes again.

"Just now," she said in a soft voice.

"Where?"

"In the same . . ." She swallowed, fingering her pearls. "In the same place as the last one."

"Where you leave the meat for your hawks?"

Miss Melody nodded silently. It was obviously painful for her to speak about it.

Jupe looked at her sympathetically.

"I know how you feel," he said. "But I'd be very grateful if you would try to answer a couple of questions."

Miss Melody nodded again. She was still playing with her pearls. The touch of them seemed to give her comfort.

"I'll try," she promised in a firmer voice.

"When we were here before," Jupe reminded her. "Edgar Allan Poe, your pet magpie . . ."

He paused. He was afraid that mentioning Miss Melody's murdered feathered friend might start her sobbing again. But she only nodded once more.

"You said he was a wonderful retriever. He brought you things."

"Pearls." Maureen Melody managed a faint smile at the fond memory. "He brought me three lovely pearls."

"You also said he was one of *two* pet magpies."

"Yes. Ralph Waldo Emerson is my other one."

"Does he bring you things too?"

"Sometimes." She slipped the handkerchief into the pocket of her dress as though determined not to weep anymore. "But I'm afraid Ralph Waldo Emerson fades in comparison to dear Edgar Allan Poe. He only brings me little bits and pieces of things. Rubbish, you know."

Jupe was frowning thoughtfully, looking at the dead hawk.

"Has he ever brought you any messages?" he asked.

"Messages?"

"Pieces of paper with writing on them."

"I don't think so. No, I'm sure I'd remember if he had. Why, this morning all he brought me—would you like to see what he brought me this morning?"

Jupe said he certainly would. Miss Melody walked over to a side table and came back with a glass ashtray. She held it out, showing it to Jupe.

Inside the ashtray was a little ball of hair. Jupe picked it up and examined it. The hair was coarse, black, and curly. Jupe figured the magpie had rolled it into a ball by worrying it with its beak. He put the hairball carefully away in his shirt pocket.

"You don't have any idea where Ralph Waldo Emerson found it, do you?" he asked.

"No, I'm afraid not." Miss Melody put the ashtray back on the table. "I can't imagine where

Edgar Allan Poe found those pearls either."

Jupe looked at the window. They still had a couple of hours before dusk.

"Come on," he suggested to Bob and Pete. "We'd better have another look through those woods." He turned to Miss Melody. "If that's all right with you."

"Of course. I'm very grateful to you and Mr. Frisbee for your help. But if you don't mind, I don't think I'll go with you. I can hardly bear to go into the garden anymore." Maureen Melody had taken out her handkerchief again. "Afraid of what I might find," she said brokenly.

She saw them out the French windows. The parrot was still perched on Pete's shoulder. He seemed to want to go with them. Pete didn't mind. He was getting to like the bird, just as he had taken to Caesar.

They stopped first at the gravel patch at the edge of the lawn where the two dead hawks had been found. There was nothing to see there, no scraps of meat, no footprints.

"Okay," Jupe sang, leading the way into the woods. "Let's keep together this time."

"Good idea," Pete sang back at the top of his voice. "Just in case we meet Frisbee in one of his bad moods."

They didn't meet anyone. For an hour the Three Investigators made their way through the shrubs and bushes, along the narrow muddy paths, without finding anything of any interest.

They emerged at last into a small grass clearing among the trees. It was strangely quiet there, as though most of the birds avoided the area. Jupe found a dry patch and sat down. He was tired and his feet were wet.

Pete sprawled beside him and Bob leaned against a tree.

They had been resting for about five minutes. Pete was absently watching a robin that was pecking the earth in search of worms. Jupe was beginning to feel it was time they pushed on.

And then suddenly three things happened. They happened so fast they all seemed to happen at once.

The parrot took off from Pete's shoulder with a terrified screech and flew into the trees.

The robin raised its head and started to spread its wings.

A black oblong shape dropped out of the sky like a bomb and landed plumb on the robin's back.

After that it was all over very quickly. The robin had no chance to struggle as the black hawk held it in its talons and tore it to pieces with its razor-sharp beak.

Within a few seconds the hawk had extracted what it wanted of the smaller bird's flesh. It took off into the sky like a rocket with its evening meal dangling from its claws. All that was left of the robin was its head and legs and a few bloodstained feathers.

None of the Three Investigators said anything for a minute. The parrot fluttered back out of the trees and perched on Pete's shoulder again.

"Cruel," the parrot said in its high-pitched voice. "Cruel. Cruel."

"You're right," Jupe agreed. "But at least we know now who, or rather what, killed the two-toed pigeon."

"And why somebody's been poisoning the hawks," Bob suggested. "I mean, maybe to keep them from killing any more homing pigeons."

"Right." Jupe pulled the little ball of black curly hair out of his pocket and looked at it. "But we still can't be sure who did poison the hawks. Or who beat Edgar Allan Poe to death with a stick." He stood up.

"Footprints," he said thoughtfully. "With all that rain last night, there have to be footprints somewhere. We've just missed them so far, that's all."

He glanced at the sun. "Come on," he said. "We've still got a good hour of daylight. We'll split up this time. Search every path, every patch of muddy ground."

"If we do come across anything," Bob asked,

"how will we signal each other this time?"

"Sing 'God Bless America' as loudly as you can," Jupe told him.

Pete practiced a couple of bars to get the tune right. He nodded. Then the Three Investigators separated and set off into the woods again in search of footprints.

It was Pete who found them, about fifteen minutes later. Two perfect shoe prints crossing the muddy path he had been following.

He stopped, looking down at them. The light was beginning to fade. With the approach of sunset the birds had grown quieter. It was sort of creepy, being here in the woods all by himself, Pete thought.

He opened his mouth to sing.

He couldn't remember the tune. He had had it perfectly back there in the clearing. But now, for the life of him, he couldn't remember how it went.

"God bless . . ." he tried. No, that wasn't right. "God bless . . ."

"God bless America," the parrot on his shoulder suddenly screeched. It had remembered the tune perfectly.

"Thanks." Pete stroked its feathers.

"God bless America," Pete sang at the top of his voice, "land that I love."

Jupe and Bob must have been quite close by. A minute later they joined him. Jupe looked at the long shoe prints, at the pointed toes. He took the little ball of hair out of his pocket and looked at that again.

"Good for you, Pete," he said. "Those certainly aren't Frisbee's footprints. I took a good look at his shoes when we were having lunch yesterday. He has very small feet and he wears blunt-toed shoes. So . . ." He held up the ball of hair. "It probably wasn't Frisbee who got his beard caught on some prickly bush and left this behind for Ralph Waldo Emerson, the magpie, to find."

He led the way out of the woods to where they had parked their bicycles. The three boys paused there in the driveway. The light was on upstairs in Maureen Melody's house. Jupe guessed that she was probably lying down and he didn't want to intrude on her sorrow.

"Anyway," he explained to the other two Investigators, "we've got nothing definite to tell her yet. Nothing but guesses."

"You think those were Blinky's footprints?" Bob asked, remembering what Jupe had said about the pointed shoes Blinky was wearing in the diner.

"That's my first guess," Jupe agreed. "My second guess is that the answer to the whole mystery lies with Kyoto."

"Why?" Pete asked.

"It was Kyoto who wrote that message, 'No

pearls today.' " Jupe held up one stubby finger and then raised a second one beside it. "It was Kyoto whom Parker Frisbee was visiting in Little Tokyo." He held up a third finger. "It was Kyoto whom Blinky was waiting for in the Seahorse Diner."

Pete nodded. "Makes sense," he agreed.

"And thanks to Bob," Jupe went on, "we know why he was waiting for him. Why he followed him."

"We do?" Bob wasn't sure he understood that.

"Because as you deduced from the wet paint on his mailbox, Kyoto had just moved into a new house. And Blinky wanted to find out where he had moved to, where Kyoto was living now."

"Why?" Bob asked.

"That's what we've got to find out," Jupe admitted. "What's Blinky's connection with Kyoto? And what's Kyoto's connection with pearls?"

He was silent for a moment. "We're going to have to follow that van again," he decided. "It's the only concrete lead we've got."

"Maybe we could tune it in on the beeper," Pete suggested.

Jupiter shook his head. "The battery on the beeper will be dead by now, and it's too risky to walk up that driveway to Kyoto's house and change it."

He looked at the Second Investigator.

"I'm afraid this is a job for you, Pete," he told him.

Pete sighed. Whenever anything looked risky, it always seemed to be a job for him.

"Okay," he said reluctantly. "Tell me what you want me to do, Jupe."

11
Kyoto's Secret

Pete got up before dawn the next morning. He put on his jeans and a gray sweater and sneakers and crept downstairs to the kitchen to get himself some breakfast.

There was a pair of dark glasses in a case on the kitchen table. His father must have left them there. Pete wondered if he ought to wear them. He pondered the question while he ate a couple of doughnuts and drank a glass of milk.

Would he look more noticeable in dark glasses or less? If Kyoto caught sight of him, would the Japanese remember and recognize him anyway?

He decided to take the glasses with him. That way he could put them on later if he wanted to change the way he looked. He clipped the case inside his sweater and went out to the shed where he kept his special bicycle.

It was an English racer with a ten-speed gear. His father had given it to him for his last birthday. Pete took very good care of it, using his old bike for ordinary, everyday transportation. He could average thirty miles an hour on the racer, with a top speed of over forty.

He patted it affectionately, the way he would have patted a horse, as he wheeled it out of the shed and swung onto the seat.

Ten minutes later he was on the edge of Little Tokyo. He parked the racer on the sidewalk among the trees where he could keep a watch on Kyoto's house without being seen.

It was okay. He had gotten here in time. The green van was still parked in the driveway and there was a light on above Kyoto's porch.

The sun was just rising when he saw a blue sedan go past and stop outside the house. A man got out of the car and walked up the driveway toward the van. Pete strained his eyes to make out the details of the man's appearance. Cutaway coat, striped trousers, heavy black beard and mustache. Parker Frisbee! Pete was sure of that. Even in the dim light he couldn't be mistaken.

Frisbee wasn't wearing his dark glasses and he was carrying a large, square package. It looked grayish in the half-light, as though it might be wrapped in newspaper. Frisbee opened the back door of the van and placed the package inside.

The light went off on Kyoto's porch.

Frisbee closed the door of the van, walked back to the blue car, got in, and drove off.

Pete settled back against the tree again to wait. Ten minutes later a Japanese man came out of the house and walked to the van. Pete had a sudden moment of indecision. Was it Kyoto or the interpreter?

Then Pete remembered what Jupe had said about the interpreter's tooled belt and the grease stain on his jeans. The man walking down the driveway had neither. It was Kyoto. He was wearing faded denims and carrying a metal lunch box.

Pete pulled his racing bike away from the trees and sat astride it.

Kyoto didn't open the rear door of the van or even glance through the rear window. He got into the front with his lunch box and started to back down the drive. Pete edged his bicycle onto the street.

At the bottom of the driveway the van backed into a right turn, stopped for a moment, and headed straight toward him. Pete lifted his bicycle hastily behind a tree.

The van rattled past him on the other side of the street. Pete counted to ten and went after it.

He had no trouble keeping the van in sight as it wound down the hill into town. Once on Main

Street he kept a safe block behind it, until it turned onto the coast road.

It picked up speed there and Pete enjoyed pushing his racer up to thirty, thirty-five, forty miles an hour, pedaling along a hundred yards behind the van in top gear. It was full daylight as he raced past the Seahorse Diner and down the hill beyond it.

A few minutes later he was passing Wills Beach. Camping was allowed on the beach as long as you didn't light fires. There were several tents on the sand. A girl came out of one of the tents and waved to Pete as he rode past.

Two miles beyond Wills Beach the road turned away from the ocean. Pete glanced over toward the distant breakers. He was thinking that it would be a great day for a swim when he was suddenly forced to jerk on his brakes and skid to a halt.

The rear red lights of the van had flashed on. Pete sat astride his bicycle, gripping the handlebars, as the van came to a dead stop.

He remembered how wiry Kyoto had looked. It crossed his mind that it was the Japanese who had invented karate. He started to lift his light racer around, ready to give up the pursuit and pedal away before it was too late.

The green van started slowly forward and turned off the highway to the left.

Pete hadn't noticed before that there was a

narrow road leading toward the sea. He pedaled cautiously forward to the junction of the turnoff. Thirty yards away the narrow road ended in a parking lot. Beyond that was a high chain-link fence with a gate in it. On the other side of the fence was a cluster of wooden huts.

The green van had pulled into the parking lot. Edging over to the side of the highway where he could take cover among the sagebrush, Pete watched Kyoto get out with his lunch box and walk around to the back of the van.

He saw the Japanese open the rear door and climb inside, closing the door after him.

He stayed in there for what seemed a long time, several minutes anyway. Pete wondered what he was doing. Changing his clothes?

No. When he came out at last Kyoto was still wearing the same denims. He was holding his lunch box in front of him with both hands as he walked toward the gate in the fence.

A man in uniform came out of one of the wooden huts. He had a gun on his hip, but he wasn't an ordinary policeman. Some kind of security guard, Pete guessed. The man opened the gate and Kyoto stepped inside. The guard closed and locked the gate again.

Pete pulled farther back among the sagebrush as a pickup truck approached along the highway and turned off down the narrow side road. There were two Japanese in the back of the truck.

Another two men got out of the cab as the truck stopped in the parking lot. They were all carrying lunch boxes. The four Japanese walked to the gate and were let in by the armed guard.

What kind of a place was it? Pete wondered. Except for the wooden huts there was nothing to be seen. Behind the fence and huts was flat land that stretched all the way to the beach and the ocean. There didn't seem to be anything growing on the land.

And then Pete saw that it wasn't land at all. It was water. It was a huge, artificial inland sea, separated from the beach by a low stone dam. The water was crisscrossed like a checkerboard by wooden causeways, slatted boardwalks a few inches above the surface.

He saw the Japanese scatter along these causeways and, crouching down, begin to haul up what looked like wire cages. He couldn't see what was in those cages, but the Japanese were squatting over them and seemed to be carefully sorting through whatever was inside.

Pete could no longer tell which of the men was Kyoto, but he could count five squatting figures so he knew Kyoto must be one of them.

He stayed hidden among the bushes for another half hour. Nothing happened. Nothing changed. Security guards patrolled the fence now and then. There were at least three of them, Pete could see now. The workers squatted patiently over their

wire cages. From time to time they lowered one
cage back into the water, hauled up another one,
and squatted over that.

Seagulls and pigeons wheeled and hovered
above the inland sea. But that was nothing
unusual. There were gulls and pigeons on every
beach along the coast.

Time to report, Pete decided at last. He had
noticed a gas station a mile back down the
highway. He pulled his bicycle out of the bushes
and rode to the filling station at top speed.

Jupe answered the phone in Headquarters at
once. Pete explained where he was, about a mile
beyond Wills Beach. He said he would wait for
the other Investigators at the gas station.

It will take them at least an hour to get here,
he figured as he left the phone booth. He bought
a soft drink and a candy bar and settled in
the shade of the station to wait.

"Nice bike." The station attendant had
wandered over and was admiring Pete's English
racer.

Pete thanked him. The attendant, who was
only a couple of years older than he was, was
something of a bicycle buff. He and Pete talked
about the various makes and the different kinds
of speed gears in a friendly way, until it occurred
to Pete that the other boy might be able to give
him some useful information.

"That place up the highway," he said. "With

the chain-link fence and the security guards. What is it?"

"From what I hear," the attendant told him, "it's an oyster farm. Some rich Japanese guy built it a few years ago. He dug out the land and flooded it with sea water and I hear they raise oysters there."

Pete didn't know whether the attendant could have told him more than that. The traffic was getting heavier and the boy was busy at the gas pumps until Jupe and Bob arrived.

Jupe was hot and out of breath after the long ride. He refused a soft drink. "Too many calories," he explained, and refreshed himself instead at the water fountain. Then Pete took his friends aside and told them everything that had happened, everything he had seen since leaving home that morning.

"An oyster farm," Jupe repeated thoughtfully when he had finished. "Security guards. Parker Frisbee. A large, square, gray package. Good work, Pete."

"Yeah, but what does it all mean, Jupe?" Pete asked.

The First Investigator didn't answer. "Let's try to find a good place to hide so we can watch what happens next," he suggested instead.

The Three Investigators biked up to the turnoff in single file. They pulled their bicycles well off the highway among the sage bushes and lay down there so they could watch the narrow side road and the gate at the end of it.

Jupe had brought binoculars with him. He focused them on the Japanese workers crouched over their wire cages.

"They're oysters, all right," he said. "In those cages. It's difficult to see through the fence and tell exactly what they're doing with them, but they seem to be opening some of the oysters."

The sun was high and blazing by now. Pete wished he had brought another can of soft drink from the gas station. He put on his dark glasses and, rolling onto his back, closed his eyes.

At noon one of the guards blew a whistle. The Japanese workers stopped for lunch. They stayed where they were on the causeways, sitting in the sun and eating out of their lunch boxes.

Gulls and pigeons strutted around them, hoping for scraps. The Japanese shooed them away. The birds finally gave up, fluttered into the air, and flew off.

Jupiter lowered his binoculars. Watching the Japanese eat had made him realize how hungry he was. He tried to force the thought of food out of his mind and concentrate on the mystery of the two-toed pigeon and the murdered birds. Unconsciously, he started pinching his lower lip.

That gray package Pete had seen Parker Frisbee put in the back of the green van. What was in it? According to Pete, Kyoto had left it in his van when he walked in through the gate with his lunch box.

Jupe nudged Pete awake.

"Did Kyoto lock the back of his van?" he asked as Pete stirred and raised his head. Jupe couldn't see if Pete's eyes were open or not because of the dark glasses, but he seemed to be more or less conscious.

"No," Pete told him sleepily. "No, I'm sure he didn't." He lowered his head and went back to sleep.

Jupe considered the possibilities. Could he creep up to the back of the green van, slip inside, and open that gray package? He was forced to admit that the answer was no. The armed guards hadn't knocked off for lunch. They were still patrolling the gate and the wire fences.

A few minutes later the whistle shrilled again. The Japanese closed their lunch boxes and went back to work, sorting through the oysters in those wire cages.

Jupe tried hard to keep his eyes open. But there was nothing to look at, even through the binoculars. Nothing new anyway. The heat and the stillness and his hunger were overcoming him. He felt his eyelids closing. His head dropped onto his hands.

He dreamed he was eating pecan pie. It had lots of whipped cream on it. He was just plunging his fork into a second slice . . .

The shrill whistle woke him up. It was three o'clock, he saw by his watch. The Japanese were lowering their wire cages back into the water. They stood up and started filing back toward the gate.

Jupe's mind was suddenly very clear after his nap. Dark glasses, he thought, and it was like a discovery. Parker Frisbee had been wearing them in Miss Melody's woods and again in the parking lot of the Trustee Bank. Both times at night. But dark glasses did more than shield your eyes from the light. They shielded them from other people. He hadn't even been able to tell just now whether Pete's eyes were open or not.

Jupe looked across at the wire fence. The Japanese weren't coming out through the gate. They were disappearing into one of the wooden huts. Then Jupe saw that all the guards had disappeared too.

He clambered quickly to his feet and ran as fast as he could across the highway and down the narrow road that led to the parking lot.

Bob opened his eyes. There was no one beside him. Where was Jupe? Where had he gone? Then, looking across the highway, he saw the First Investigator open the back of the van and climb inside. The van door closed.

"Oh no." Pete raised his head.

"What do you think we ought to do?" Bob asked him. "I mean what do you think Jupe wants us to do? You think he's going to try to hide in Kyoto's van and ride back with him? Or what?"

"I don't know." Pete sounded as puzzled as Bob. "But if he wanted us to do anything, he'd have told us, wouldn't he?"

"Yes. Maybe he's just searching the van. We'd better wait for him here, I guess. I only hope he gets back before Kyoto . . ." He had been going to say, "Before Kyoto catches him." But there was no sign of Kyoto or anyone else. No Japanese. No guards.

Bob picked up the binoculars and swept them over the empty causeways, the chain-link fence. He paused, focusing on the window of one of the huts.

It was difficult to make out anything very clearly, but he could see that the hut was full of guards and Japanese. The Japanese had taken their clothes off. The guards seemed to be searching them, searching through their clothes, searching inside their lunch boxes.

Bob lowered the binoculars. Jupe was running back toward him across the highway. The First Investigator flopped down beside him in the sagebrush. Jupe was red-faced and panting, but there was a gleam of excitement in his eyes.

"The guards are searching them, aren't they?" he asked as soon as he had recovered his breath.

Bob nodded. "That's what it looks like anyway. What do you think they're looking for, Jupe?"

The First Investigator didn't answer that at once. "I did some searching myself," he said after a moment. "I found out what was in that package in Kyoto's van. But that wasn't newspaper it was wrapped in, Pete. I guess it just looked like it, sort of gray, in the pale light. It was actually cheesecloth."

"Cheesecloth," Pete said. "You mean like Blinky's package?"

"Exactly like it," Jupe answered. "The cloth had been stripped away. But the cage was still there in the back of the van. The cage is empty now. But I bet it wasn't empty this morning when Frisbee put it in the van. Because I found this in it."

He held up his hand, showing his two friends what he had found. It was a grain of corn.

"Pigeons," Pete said. "Kyoto had a pigeon in that cage . . ."

"And he smuggled it in through the gate in his lunch box," Jupe went on. "That was easy enough. The guards don't search the Japanese workers when they go in. Only when they come out."

Bob was frowning, puzzled. "But what are they searching them for?" he asked again.

"Pearls," Jupe explained patiently. "That's what all those oysters are for. It's a cultured pearl farm."

12
Jupe Has a Plan

"Pearls," Jupiter said again. "Pearls and homing pigeons."

The Three Investigators had met back at Headquarters after leaving the oyster farm. They were all eating sandwiches that Aunt Mathilda had made for them. Jupe had cut his sandwich in two. He had made up his mind to eat only half of it.

Bob had been the last to arrive. He had stopped off at the library for two books Jupe had asked him to get.

"What does it say about cultured pearls?" Jupe asked him.

Bob opened one of the books, titled *Precious*

Gems. He took out a sheet of paper on which he had made some notes.

"Cultured pearls." He settled his glasses on his nose. "You take baby oysters, called spat, and collect them in cages under water. When the oysters are three years old, you open them up and put a tiny grain of mother-of-pearl inside the shell. You put it into what's known as the mantle of the oyster. Then you lower the cages back under water. Leave the oysters there for anywhere from three to six years, opening and examining them now and then. The oysters are irritated by the little speck of hard matter that's been put inside them and they form a pearl around it like . . ."

"Like a sort of bandage," Pete suggested.

"Yes, well, like a sort of protection, anyway." Bob went back to his notes. "After about six years the pearls are fully grown and you take them out of the oysters and match them and sell them. It's a big industry in Japan. Some cultured pearls are worth several hundred dollars."

"Why are they called cultured?" asked Pete. "Do the oysters go to the opera or something?"

Bob and Jupiter groaned at the Second Investigator's bad joke.

"No, no," said Bob. "Cultured here means raised, or grown artificially. You try to make sure a pearl starts growing by putting a hard speck into the oyster. You don't just wait for a bit of grit to get into the oyster by accident."

"So they're growing pearls at that place where Kyoto works." Pete was stroking Caesar's feathers through the chicken wire of his big cage. "And that's why the guards search the workers when they're leaving. To stop them from stealing any of the pearls. Right, Jupe?"

"Right." The First Investigator leaned back in his swivel chair. "But they don't search them when they go in through the gate. And that gave Parker Frisbee and Kyoto an idea. A very simple idea. That's the beauty of it. Parker Frisbee puts a caged homing pigeon in the back of Kyoto's van. When he gets to the oyster farm, Kyoto takes the pigeon out of the cage and smuggles it in inside his lunch box."

Jupe was silent for a minute, fiddling with the second half of his sandwich. He pushed it away from him.

"If Kyoto finds a good pearl in one of the oysters that day, he waits until his lunch hour, takes the pigeon out of his lunch box, and fastens the pearl to its leg. There are so many birds around that place that none of the guards is going to notice one more. The pigeon flies off home to Parker Frisbee's pigeon coop and delivers the pearl to him."

"And if Kyoto doesn't happen to come across a good pearl before lunchtime," Bob said, "he sends

Parker Frisbee a message in Japanese: 'No pearls today.' Like the message we found on that two-toed pigeon that got killed by Miss Melody's hawks. But . . ."

He paused, trying to figure it out. "But . . ." he repeated in a puzzled voice.

"But that pigeon didn't belong to Parker Frisbee," Jupe finished for him. "It belonged to Blinky. At least Blinky had it with him in the Seahorse Diner. In exactly the same kind of cage wrapped in cheesecloth."

Without thinking about what he was doing, Jupe broke off a piece of the sandwich. "Let's have a look at that other book, Bob," he said.

The second book Bob had brought from the library was a road atlas of southern California. Jupe put the piece of sandwich in his mouth to free his hands and opened the atlas to the small-scale map that included Rocky Beach and Santa Monica. The other two Investigators leaned over his shoulder to look at it.

"Now here's Wills Beach." Jupe put his stubby finger on the map on a section of coastline that stretched east to west. "So the oyster farm must be here. And Parker Frisbee lives . . ." He moved his finger down the coast to Rocky Beach, chewing absent-mindedly. "Here. On the west side of town. I know because I looked up his home address in the phone book."

He took a ruler from his desk and laid it between the two points. "So what does that tell us?" he asked.

"It's a clear flight, mainly over the ocean, between the oyster farm and Frisbee's house, where he probably keeps his pigeon coop," Pete answered. "About six miles."

"Which would take a racing pigeon about six minutes," Bob said. "So all Frisbee has to do is go home at noon and he doesn't have long to wait for his pigeon and his pearl."

"But then how did the pigeon get killed in Miss Melody's woods?" Pete objected. "Maureen Melody lives on the east side of town." He pointed on the map. "That's way beyond Frisbee's place. What was that two-toed pigeon doing so far off course?"

"It was only off course if it was going to Frisbee's coop." Jupe moved the ruler so that it lay along a line between the oyster farm and Miss Melody's house. "But not if it was going here." He put his finger on the map, pointing to a town a few miles down the coast from Rocky Beach.

"Santa Monica," Bob said.

"Blinky?" Pete suggested.

"Blinky lives in Santa Monica," Bob remembered. "He admitted that in the Seahorse Diner . . ."

"So if that two-toed pigeon belonged to Blinky," Jupe continued, "and it was flying back to Blinky's coop in Santa Monica, it would fly over Maureen Melody's woods. And that's how it got killed by one of her hawks."

He was silent again for a moment, thoughtfully fingering what was left of the sandwich.

"And obviously it wasn't the first of Blinky's pigeons to get killed that way," he went on. "Miss Melody said Edgar Allan Poe had brought her three pearls this month. It seems to me highly probable that the magpie had found all those pearls attached to the legs of dead pigeons in Miss Melody's woods."

"It seems to fit," Pete agreed.

Jupe frowned, closing the atlas.

"It might fit," he said, "if Frisbee and Blinky are partners. That is, if they use one of Blinky's homing pigeons one day and one of Frisbee's the next. That's the only way Parker Frisbee's behavior makes any sense. He's worried about Blinky's birds getting killed. He searches Miss Melody's woods at night. He sees me there and he thinks I'm the killer. He attacks me with a stick."

Jupe broke off another piece of the sandwich.

"Then he hears from Maureen Melody that we're trying to help her. So he decides to be friendly. He offers us a reward to find out what's happening to Blinky's pigeons."

He shook his head, frowning at the bread and cheese he was holding in his fingers. The sight of it seemed to distract him. He put it in his mouth.

"But they can't be partners," he said.

"Why not?" Bob asked. "What makes you think they're not?"

Jupe chewed for a moment before answering. "If they're partners," he pointed out, "then Blinky and Kyoto are partners too." Jupe was absent-mindedly fingering another fragment of sandwich, like a dog worrying a bone. "And Blinky would know where Kyoto lived. He would know where his new house was. He wouldn't have to wait in the Seahorse Diner to follow Kyoto's green van home from work to find out where he'd moved to."

Jupe stood up, putting the fragment in his mouth, as though to get it out of his sight. He looked at Bob and Pete. "I vote we all get permission from our folks to spend the night on Wills Beach," he said.

He knew there would be no difficulty about that. The Three Investigators often went camping in the summertime. They arranged to meet back at the salvage yard in two hours. Jupe would ask Hans, one of Uncle Titus' helpers, to drive them all to Wills Beach in his truck with their bicycles and sleeping bags.

"Then early tomorrow morning," Jupiter said, "when Kyoto comes along, going to the oyster farm in his green van, we'll be ready for him."

"What are we going to do?" Pete asked. "Follow him again?"

"No." Jupe shook his head. "We're going to try to solve this case, once and for all, in a simple, practical way."

He looked at his desk, searching for the half sandwich he had intended to save for his supper later. It wasn't there. He realized with a pang that he had eaten it all without meaning to.

"We're going to use Caesar to trap Blinky!" he said.

13
The Big Switch

He was not really the outdoor type, Jupiter decided when he woke up in his sleeping bag the next morning. He was stiff from lying on the hard beach all night and his eyes and mouth felt full of sand.

He looked at his watch. Six o'clock. Time to get started. He stretched and crawled out of his sleeping bag.

The other two Investigators were already up. Pete was crouching over Caesar's small cage, stroking the bird's feathers while he fed it. Bob offered Jupe doughnuts and a carton of milk.

Jupe hesitated. Why not, he thought. One doughnut couldn't be all that fattening. And he needed his strength. He drank the milk slowly. It helped wash the taste of sand out of his mouth.

Ten minutes later the boys had their gear packed. Jupe helped Pete wrap Caesar's cage in cheesecloth and tape the corners shut. Then they strapped it onto the carrier of Jupe's bicycle. Pete slung an airline bag over the handlebars of his bike.

Balancing their rolled sleeping bags on their handlebars, they rode slowly up the highway to the gas station, where Pete arranged with the friendly attendant to leave their gear for a couple of hours.

They mounted up again and rode on for half a mile toward the oyster farm. Jupe had remembered a good place for his plan from the day before. The two lanes of the divided highway were separated by a wide grassy bank as they curved into a sharp bend, and there was plenty of sagebrush off to the right of the road, on the side away from the ocean.

The boys pulled their bicycles clear of the road and hid them among the bushes. Jupe unfastened Caesar's wrapped cage from his carrier and put it out of sight in the shade. Bob took the airline bag off the handlebars of his own bike. They were all carrying their bicycle pumps as they walked on around the bend in the highway. They settled down there beside the road.

Bob opened his bag and took out a party-sized sack of large balloons of all shapes and colors. He divided the balloons among the three of them, twenty each, and they set to work. Using their bicycle pumps to inflate them and tying each end shut, the boys soon had a huge mass of big, bright balloons, piled up like a tower on the edge of the highway.

Jupe had been glad to find that not a single car had passed them since they had started to work on the balloons. There was almost no traffic on this stretch of the highway so early in the morning. And working in their favor was the lack of any wind so far that day.

Bob opened his bag again and took out a folded white cloth banner he had prepared the evening before to Jupe's instructions. The boys stretched it between two bushes on the side of the road. In big red letters it said:

HELP OUR FEATHERED FRIENDS.
BUY A BALLOON.

Jupe glanced back toward the sharp bend in the highway twenty yards away, then above him to where the sage and mesquite rose on a small hill.

"You hide up there, Bob," he said. "Where you can see both Pete and me. Do you have your handkerchief?"

"Yeah." Bob took it out of the pocket of his jeans. "I'll wave it like this, Pete," Bob said.

"Backward and forward. Then you'll know it's okay to let him pass."

Pete nodded reluctantly. His insides felt all funny. He just hoped he could pull it off without making Kyoto too angry. For all he knew the young Japanese might be a black belt karate champion. If Kyoto recognized him from the salvage yard and suspected that Pete was playing a trick on him, he might go into action chopping away with both hands.

Pete took his father's dark glasses out of his pocket and put them on. "How will I know when he's coming?" he asked a little shakily.

"Three whistles means the van has just come into sight," Jupe told him. "Then I'll give two more whistles after it has passed me. Okay?"

"Okay."

Jupe noticed the uncertainty in Pete's voice. He knew Pete had the hardest part to play in the scheme he had thought up and he wished he could take his place and do it himself. But Jupe was the one Kyoto had been looking at most of the time that day at the junkyard. Jupe was the one he was most likely to remember and recognize.

"Just keep smiling, Pete," he said, trying to reassure his friend. "Just keep smiling and talking."

"What'll I say?"

"Anything," Jupe told him. "It doesn't matter.

He doesn't speak any English, so he won't understand what you're saying anyway."

"Okay," Pete repeated. But he still felt funny inside.

Jupe glanced at his watch. It was almost zero hour. "Time to go," he said.

Bob climbed to the top of the small hill and lay down in the sage there, holding his handkerchief ready.

Jupe walked back to where they had left their bicycles and hid in the bushes on the edge of the highway. Keeping one hand on the square box beside him, he could feel Caesar moving about in his cage under the cheesecloth.

Pete stayed where he was beside the enormous pile of balloons. "Help our feathered friends," he muttered, looking at the big red-lettered banner. "Never mind our feathered friends. I'm the one who needs help."

Although it was quite cool and he was lying still, Jupe could feel the sweat running down his cheeks and tickling his nose. He was worried about Pete and he couldn't even watch out for him. Both of the other two Investigators were out of sight now. Jupe kept his eyes fixed on the highway to his left, waiting for the green van.

Five minutes. Ten minutes. He was beginning to think it wasn't coming. Something had kept Kyoto from going to work this morning. Thinking of Pete, Jupe almost wished the van would never show up.

Then suddenly there it was, rattling toward him. Jupe put his fingers in his mouth and whistled three times.

The van passed him. Jupe whistled again twice.

As soon as the van was out of sight around the bend, he jumped to his feet, holding the square box against his chest, and ran along the shoulder of the highway after it.

Pete heard the first three whistles. He stretched his arms around the tower of balloons and toppled it forward across the road. By the time he heard the second two whistles he was up to his neck in the balloons, gathering them together, piling them into a bobbing, brightly colored wall across the highway.

He could hear the van approaching now. It was slowing. It came to an uncertain stop five yards from the balloon barrier Pete had constructed.

Kyoto leaned out of the window and shouted something at Pete in Japanese. Pete paid no attention. He pretended to be trying to clear the balloons out of the way, but what he was really doing was making sure there was no gap in the barrier, no way the van could pass without being smothered in a swirling sea of balloons.

Kyoto climbed out of the cab and walked toward him. He halted, looking at Pete in a puzzled way. He kicked at the nearest balloon. It was a long, green, sausage-shaped one. It bounced up and hit him gently on the nose. Kyoto said something unintelligible and pushed the balloon away from him.

Pete stretched his face into a forced smile. "Help our feathered friends," he said. "Buy a balloon."

Kyoto muttered something in Japanese.

Pete continued to smile. Just keep talking, Jupe had advised him. The trouble was he couldn't think of anything to say and his face felt as though it had been stretched into the same meaningless grin for hours. All of a sudden something popped into Pete's head. It was an old union song his father sang around the house.

"We shall not," Pete told Kyoto hopefully, "we shall not be moved." He cleared his throat and kept smiling. "We shall not, we shall not be moved. Just like a tree that's standing by the water, we shall not be moved."

Kyoto kicked at another balloon, a round yellow one this time. It rose a few feet in the air and settled on top of the others, making the barrier even higher.

"We will stand and fight together," Pete explained with a wide smile, pointing at the feathered friends banner. "We shall not be moved. We shall stand and . . ."

Jupe was only ten yards from the back of the

halted van now, running along the edge of the highway. He swerved onto the surface of the road. His sneakers made no sound as he ran the last few yards. The tricky part was going to be opening the van's rear door without Kyoto hearing him. He thanked his lucky stars that the Japanese had left his engine running.

". . . Fight together. We shall not be moved." Pete's voice rose slightly. Kyoto was fumbling in the pocket of his jeans. Fumbling for what? Pete's smile was getting a little desperate. "Just like a tree that's standing by the water," he continued hastily.

Jupe reached out and slowly, cautiously turned the handle of the rear door of the van. It squeaked. It was only a small squeak, but it sounded as loud as a scream to Jupe. He pulled the door open.

From his hiding place on the hill Bob saw Jupe lean forward and peer into the back of the van. He clutched his handkerchief more tightly.

There it was, Jupe saw, sitting in the back of the van. The square box wrapped in cheesecloth. Jupe set his own box beside it and softly, carefully lifted out the first one. Holding Kyoto's box against his chest, he shifted Caesar in his identically wrapped cage to the spot where the first box had been.

"We shall not be moved—" Pete broke off. His voice seemed to curl up and die in his throat.

Kyoto had pulled a knife out of his pocket. He opened its long, sharp, shining blade.

Jupe reached out to close the van door. There was a sudden loud, explosive bang. Jupe leaped up as though something had exploded under his own feet. The pigeon he was holding made a muffled chirp. Jupe landed and stood quite still, waiting.

There was another bang.

"Shall not be moved," Pete repeated weakly.

Kyoto was wading in among the balloons, slashing and stabbing away at them with his knife, popping one after another of them.

"The union is behind us, we shall not," Pete shouted at him with a ghastly, frozen smile, "be moved. The union is behind us . . ."

Jupe swung the door of the van gently closed. He made sure the latch had caught. He began to back away down the highway clutching Kyoto's box against his chest.

"We shall not be moved!" Pete yelled, running among the balloons like a hen trying to save its chicks from a fox. As he darted around, clutching at them, yelling "We shall not be moved," he kept glancing desperately toward the little hill where Bob was hiding.

Kyoto was still stabbing and cutting away at the balloons. He had exploded more than half of them by now.

Bob watched Jupe backing away from the van. He saw Jupe spin around, run another few yards, and plunge into the bushes on the side of the road.

Bob sat up, wildly waving his handkerchief back and forth.

"Just like a tree," Pete continued hopelessly. Then he saw the signal. Almost collapsing with relief, he watched Kyoto explode the last few balloons. He watched the Japanese walk back to his van. He saw him climb in behind the wheel.

Pete staggered to the side of the road and sat down on the bank, watching the van rumble over the punctured, deflated, brightly colored skins of the balloons. He sighed and lowered his head onto his knees.

Jupe climbed out of the bushes with Kyoto's box and walked toward Pete. He had brought it off, done what he had set out to do, switched one pigeon for the other. But he was far from pleased with himself. It was Pete, he knew, who had done the difficult, dangerous part, stopped the van and kept it halted long enough for Jupe to make the switch.

"Are you okay?" he asked, standing beside his friend, as Bob came down the hill and joined them. "You did a great job, Pete. Are you okay?"

Pete shook his head slowly from side to side. "Wh-e-w," he said. "When he pulled that knife out. My nerves will never be the same again."

He looked up at Jupiter. "Like that Poe guy said in his bird poem, never more. Never more!"

14
A Tense Homecoming

Jupiter stood crestfallen by the highway. He really was sorry that he had put Pete through such a strain. And Bob too. But at the same time he couldn't help feeling a little lift of triumph.

"At least it worked," he said after a moment. "Kyoto's gone off to the pearl oyster farm with Caesar in the back of his van."

"Okay." Pete sighed. "It worked. So what's next?"

Jupe was already untaping the cheesecloth. He lifted it aside, displaying the square cage.

"Give me a hand, will you, Bob?" he asked.

Together they opened the door of the cage and carefully lifted out the racing homer inside. Bob held the pigeon in both hands while Jupe took a small strip of aluminum tape and a Three Investigators card from his pocket. He folded the card and bent the aluminum securely around it. Then he fastened the metal tape around the pigeon's leg.

"Would you like to let it go, Pete?" Jupe asked. He thought the best way to stop Pete from worrying about his nerves was to give him something to do.

The Second Investigator nodded and Bob handed him the pigeon. Pete stood up, holding it in both hands and gently stroking its feathers with the tips of his fingers. "Time to head for home," Pete told it. He tossed the pigeon gently into the air. For several seconds it fluttered and wheeled overhead. "It's getting its bearings," Pete explained. "There it goes. Now."

He was right. The pigeon was taking off like a rocket, heading back down the coast.

Almost two hours later the Three Investigators wheeled their bicycles into the salvage yard. They had picked up their gear at the gas station on the way and, hampered by their rolled sleeping bags, had had to bicycle very slowly.

"So there you are," Aunt Mathilda greeted them. "I was afraid you were going to spend all day at the beach. Uncle Titus just brought in this load . . ."

Uncle Titus had brought in a load of old hinges. They all had to be sorted and stowed away.

Jupe sighed. But he wasn't really sorry to have to work. It was still over two hours until noon. Sorting hinges would help pass the time and give the Three Investigators an excuse for being around the yard.

The boys started the job with tense impatience. Their minds, and sometimes their eyes, were in the sky above them. Their ears were already listening for the flutter of a pigeon's wings.

At eleven thirty Uncle Titus drove Aunt Mathilda into town for her shopping. Jupe knew they wouldn't be back before two. The three boys had the whole yard to themselves until then.

They began to relax on the job. They worked more and more slowly. By noon they had given up any pretense of sorting hinges. They sat down on the ground in Jupe's outdoor workshop, craning their necks, watching the sky. Waiting.

Jupe kept glancing at his watch. Pete jumped to his feet as a swallow darted overhead and then sat down again, looking slightly sheepish.

"Of course we don't know exactly when Kyoto will let Caesar loose." Jupe was talking as much to reassure himself as the others. "He might eat his lunch first or—"

He broke off. Pete was on his feet again. And then Jupe saw it too. The beautiful, sleek, glossy bird, hovering and wheeling high above them.

"It's Caesar!" Pete waved at the pigeon.

"Caesar," he called. "Caesar. Caesar."

Caesar had seen him. He came in low, pulled out of his dive with a backward flap of his wings, and settled gracefully on his feet in the center of the workshop.

Pete was the first to reach him. He picked up the pigeon in both hands and gently stroked its neck.

"Caesar," he whispered gratefully. "Good old Caesar. You came home."

Jupe was already examining the pigeon's legs. "Wow," he cried excitedly. "Look. Look." He carefully detached the thin metal band from Caesar's ankle. Unfolding it, he lifted out what was inside. He held it out to his friends, showing them what he had found.

A large, glistening pearl.

"I guess that proves it, all right," Jupe said. He held the pearl up between his fingers. "Our whole theory about Kyoto and Parker Frisbee and the two-toed pigeon and—"

"I'll take that."

The voice had come from the entrance to the workshop area.

The Three Investigators turned to face it as though a giant hand had spun them around.

A man was standing in the opening between the tall piles of junk bordering the workshop. He was wearing a black slicker and dark glasses. It was difficult to see much more of his face because of the black bushy beard and mustache that covered it.

He moved slowly toward the boys, his right hand held out in front of him. Gripped in his hand was a long-barreled, nickel-plated gun.

It seemed to Pete that the gun was pointing straight at him. His nerves had stood all they could for one day. Without even thinking of what he was doing, he backed aside toward the fence.

The man continued to advance on Jupe. "Give it to me," he said. "That pearl."

Luckily for Jupe's nerves he wasn't looking at the gun. He was examining the man's feet. Without a second's hesitation he popped the pearl into his mouth and flipped it into his cheek with the tip of his tongue.

"If you come any closer, I'll swallow it," the First Investigator said in a slightly garbled but surprisingly calm voice.

The man's hand was trembling. With a sudden, almost frightened lurch, he threw himself at Jupe, reaching for his throat as though to choke the pearl out of him.

Bob moved quickly forward and tried to seize the man by the shoulders and pull him off Jupe.

Pete backed away another step and almost tripped over a broom.

Holding Jupe by the throat with one hand, the man jabbed backward at Bob with the other, catching him in the chest with the butt of the gun. Bob winced with pain but held on to one shoulder of the man's slicker.

Jupe struggled as the man's grip around his throat tightened. But he kept his mouth closed and the pearl firmly in his cheek.

"Duck, Bob!" cried Pete.

The Second Investigator had recovered his nerve. Bob ducked just in time as Pete swung the broom in a wide arc and hit the man hard across the back of the neck with it.

The man slumped to his knees. The gun dropped from his hand. His dark glasses fell off.

"Oh well, you can't win them all," he said. It was funny the way he said it because as soon as he had spoken the last word he winked. He kept on winking as Jupe stooped and picked up the gun.

"Is it loaded?" the First Investigator asked.

"No. No, of course not. I'm scared stiff of guns."

The man's right eye was opening and closing now in an absolute spasm of winking. It was obvious that he couldn't help it. It was a nervous tic. He climbed weakly to his feet and moved toward Jupe. Pete half raised the broom.

"It's okay," the man told him. "I'm sick of the whole business anyway. I never would have started it except that I'd been playing the horses and losing and I had to make some quick dough somehow."

"You'd have made more money if it hadn't been

for Maureen Melody's hawks," Jupe said. "I guess we were lucky that your pigeon with our card attached to it got safely past her woods today."

The First Investigator took the pearl out of his mouth and put it carefully away in his pocket. He felt rather sorry for the man. He looked so nervous and sweaty in his heavy black slicker. And he must have been awfully uncomfortable wearing all that bushy hair on his face on a hot day like this.

"Why don't you take it off," he suggested kindly. "I mean that false beard."

"Might as well," Blinky agreed.

He looked sort of naked and helpless without it. He no longer looked like Parker Frisbee at all, especially after Jupe had helped him off with the slicker that disguised how much thinner than Frisbee he was.

He stood there winking incessantly in the sunlight while Bob and Pete kept a watch on him and Jupe went into Headquarters to call Chief Reynolds at the police station and tell him the whole story.

15
Don's Revenge

"Blinky admitted everything and Chief Reynolds arrested all three of them," Jupe said. "He locked up Parker Frisbee and Kyoto and Blinky. Frisbee and Kyoto are out on bail. But Blinky says he'd sooner stay locked up. It keeps him from playing the horses, and I guess he's also a little scared of what Frisbee and Kyoto might do to him for horning in on their little pearl-stealing racket."

The Three Investigators were sitting around the patio table in Hector Sebastian's huge living room. They had been telling him the story of the pearls and the pigeons. Sebastian smoked a pipe while he listened and asked an occasional question.

"How did Blinky catch on to what they were doing?" he inquired.

"He used to work for Parker Frisbee," Bob explained, "looking after Frisbee's pigeons and helping out in the store. Until Frisbee fired him for dipping into the petty cash. By then Blinky had seen enough of Frisbee's business to know that he was getting cultured pearls from some illegal source."

"So after Frisbee fired him," Pete went on, "Blinky tailed him until he found out exactly what he was doing."

"Putting his homing pigeons in the back of Kyoto's van." Hector Sebastian took the pipe out of his mouth and gave a small cough. "And that gave Blinky the idea that two could play the same game. All he needed was a few homing pigeons of his own. Right, Jupe?"

The First Investigator nodded. "Blinky had two things going for him. One was that Parker Frisbee was a shrewd businessman and not too greedy. He only put a pigeon in the van a few times a week. Mostly on regular days. Sometimes in the morning. And sometimes the evening before. Kyoto would check his van for a pigeon every day, just to be sure. Frisbee had as little contact with Kyoto as possible. He paid him once a month by putting an envelope of cash under the cheesecloth around the pigeon cage. So he didn't have to see Kyoto or be seen with him . . ."

"Unless something went wrong," Bob put in. "Like when we showed up with Caesar at the jewelry store. Frisbee had to talk to Kyoto about that. That's why we met Parker Frisbee coming out of Kyoto's house that day."

"And he bought you all a delicious Japanese lunch." The mystery writer put the pipe back in his mouth and puffed on it without any apparent enjoyment. "What was the second thing Blinky had going for him, Jupe?" he asked.

"The fact that Kyoto was Japanese," Jupe explained. "To Kyoto all short, slightly stout Americans with bushy black beards looked alike. Especially when he only saw them at a distance under his porch light. With a false beard, and a slicker to make him look heavier, Blinky could walk up the driveway and put his own pigeons in the van and Kyoto would think he was Frisbee."

"As long as he picked the off days when Frisbee wouldn't be doing it." Sebastian coughed again, putting his pipe down on the table.

"Exactly," Jupe agreed. "And for quite a long time it worked. Everything was going fine for Blinky. He was getting his own pigeons back with a pearl fastened to their legs. Until Maureen Melody's hawks started killing his birds."

"I suppose he knew Miss Melody, or at least knew about her, from working for Frisbee." Sebastian picked up his pipe. "And he figured out, just as you did, that his pigeons were flying over her woods on the way back to Santa Monica. So he started poisoning her hawks."

"And then something else went wrong for Blinky." Jupe looked at Bob. "Why don't you continue the story. It was because you noticed the wet paint on the mailbox that we were able to fit that piece into place."

"Blinky was in big trouble the day we met him in the Seahorse Diner," Bob said, taking over from Jupe. "He was in debt to his bookie and he was absolutely desperate. He'd gone to Kyoto's house that morning to put his pigeon in the green van. And the van wasn't there. The house was closed. Kyoto had moved. So Blinky decided to wait for him on the highway and tail him home from work. He still had his two-toed pigeon with him and he was so nervous he forgot it when he ran out of the diner to follow Kyoto's van."

"That's the part that puzzles me." Sebastian relit his pipe with a slight frown of distaste. "What did Blinky do then? Why did he switch Caesar for his two-toed pigeon in the salvage yard?"

"We only know this from what Blinky told Chief Reynolds," Jupe answered. "He tailed Kyoto to his new house and, just to make sure Kyoto *was* living there, he kept a watch on the place that evening. After a while he saw Frisbee walk up Kyoto's driveway and put his usual square package in the back of Kyoto's van. Blinky wasn't expecting that. It was the wrong day for Frisbee. But Frisbee had switched days that week because Kyoto had taken a vacation the day before to move houses. As Bob said, Blinky was desperate. He waited until Kyoto's lights went off and then stole Frisbee's pigeon out of the back of the van. He had already phoned the waitress at the diner and found out that we had gone off with the package he had left there. So he came after us to get it back."

"And someone told him where you lived, at the Jones Salvage Yard." Hector Sebastian puffed out a cloud of smoke.

"And that's when Blinky got a break," Pete said. "There was his own two-toed pigeon in a big chicken-wire cage, right out in the yard. His problem then was, what was he going to do with Caesar, Frisbee's pigeon?"

"He couldn't set him free," Jupe pointed out. "If he had, Caesar would have flown straight home to Parker Frisbee that night. And Frisbee would have gone around to Kyoto to see what was wrong."

"So he left Caesar with you in the chicken-wire coop," the mystery writer said. "And put his own two-toed pigeon in Frisbee's cage, then replaced it in Kyoto's van."

"Right," Jupe agreed. "Then Blinky went home to wait for his pigeon and his pearl. Only his bird didn't show up at noon the next day. Miss Melody's hawks had killed it."

"That's the creepy part in a way," Bob said.

"Blinky must have been in Maureen Melody's woods, poisoning her hawk, at the very time we were paying our first visit to her. He must have seen us walk into her living room with Caesar. He must also have seen Miss Melody's pet magpie, Edgar Allan Poe, go hopping in after us with a pearl in his beak."

"And that was too much for him." Hector Sebastian's wry laughter turned into a cough. He put his pipe back on the table. "Foolish Blinky. He lost his head altogether then. He was so angry at the magpie that he beat it to death."

"Blinky was still there in the woods when we left," Jupe said. "He saw us go off down the drive with Caesar. And when he followed us, he must have gotten really scared. Because we went straight to Parker Frisbee's jewelry store."

"Blinky's black car was parked in the street when we came out," Pete remembered. "And of course we still had Caesar with us."

"Blinky must have been really confused then," Sebastian suggested. "He didn't know what you'd told Parker Frisbee or what Frisbee had told you."

"Frisbee didn't tell us anything," Jupe pointed out. "He was too smart to let us know Caesar was his bird. He pretended he didn't know who Caesar belonged to. And then tried to put us off the scent by telling us he was a hen pigeon and not a racing homer at all."

"If Blinky had been half as smart," Sebastian agreed, "he would have played it cool too."

"He just couldn't. He was too nervous," Bob said. "He wanted to throw our suspicion on Frisbee and at the same time keep Frisbee quiet by letting Caesar fly back to him. So he phoned us, put on his false beard and his slicker, and held Jupe up in the parking lot, taking Caesar away with him."

"I must say he fooled me," Jupe admitted. "Of course it was half dark and I only saw his face for a second. But I really did think it was Parker Frisbee with that gun. Just as I thought it was Frisbee who had attacked me in the woods."

"When did you begin to suspect it wasn't?" the mystery writer asked. "What made you think it might be Blinky in disguise?"

"It was partly that the bearded man panicked so quickly when I shone my bicycle light on him in the woods," Jupe said. "And later we found what looked like Blinky's footprints there. But it was mostly thanks to Pete that I made the connection. The afternoon when we were hiding beside the highway, watching the oyster farm, Pete was wearing dark glasses. And I suddenly realized I couldn't see his eyes through them. That was the one thing Blinky couldn't disguise. His winking eye. So he had to wear dark glasses to hide it. Even at night."

Hector Sebastian picked up his pipe. He sniffed

and then put it reluctantly in his mouth. "And how's Maureen Melody these days?" he asked. "Happy as a lark, I suppose."

"Yes," Pete said, smiling. "At least nobody's poisoning her hawks anymore. But she does complain that Ralph Waldo Emerson never brings her any pearls. I don't think that Frisbee's crooked scheme has quite registered with her."

The mystery writer puffed away in silence for a minute until he started coughing again. "I hate this pipe," he said. "But I have to smoke it, whether I like it or not."

"Why?" Jupe was puzzled.

"Because of the smell in here. Haven't you noticed the smell?"

Bob breathed in deeply through his nose. There was a faint aroma from the kitchen. But it seemed a pleasant one to him. Like good food cooking. "What smell?" he asked.

"Oh, you'll see," Hector Sebastian told him. "Don will be bringing in our lunch soon and you'll see what I mean." He sighed nostalgically. "Oh, for some seaweed."

The Vietnamese houseman came in a few minutes later, holding an enormous tray of food above his head. He was wearing a gauze mask over his mouth and nose. He set the tray down on the table.

"Your favorite food, Mr. Sebastian," he said. "Yes?"

"No," Hector Sebastian said glumly, sighing again. "He's punishing me for my greediness," he explained to the boys.

Pete pulled his chair closer to the table. Some punishment, he thought. "It looks delicious," he said.

"Not if you have it for breakfast, lunch, and dinner," Sebastian protested. "And Don has threatened me with a whole week of it. Three times a day."

He put his pipe in his mouth. "That's why I have to smoke this thing," he said. "It's the only way I can get the smell of fried food out of my nose."

He looked at the Vietnamese. "That horrible, disgusting smell. Isn't that what you called it, Don?"

Don sniffed through his surgical mask.

"What smell?" he asked, serving the ham and eggs and sausages and french fries. "I smell nothing. Not even pipe."

Jupe looked at the heaped plate of food in front of him. "Not for me, thank you," he said. He pushed the plate away regretfully.

"I'm on a diet," the First Investigator explained. "So I won't have anything at all, thank you." Jupe smiled politely at the Vietnamese houseman.

"Unless you happen to have some good, unfattening seaweed handy," he added.

THE THREE INVESTIGATORS MYSTERY SERIES

NOVELS

The Secret of Terror Castle
The Mystery of the Stuttering Parrot
The Mystery of the Whispering Mummy
The Mystery of the Green Ghost
The Mystery of the Vanishing Treasure
The Secret of Skeleton Island
The Mystery of the Fiery Eye
The Mystery of the Silver Spider
The Mystery of the Screaming Clock
The Mystery of the Moaning Cave
The Mystery of the Talking Skull
The Mystery of the Laughing Shadow
The Secret of the Crooked Cat
The Mystery of the Coughing Dragon
The Mystery of the Flaming Footprints
The Mystery of the Nervous Lion
The Mystery of the Singing Serpent
The Mystery of the Shrinking House
The Secret of Phantom Lake
The Mystery of Monster Mountain
The Secret of the Haunted Mirror
The Mystery of the Dead Man's Riddle
The Mystery of the Invisible Dog
The Mystery of Death Trap Mine
The Mystery of the Dancing Devil
The Mystery of the Headless Horse
The Mystery of the Magic Circle
The Mystery of the Deadly Double
The Mystery of the Sinister Scarecrow
The Secret of Shark Reef
The Mystery of the Scar-Faced Beggar
The Mystery of the Blazing Cliffs

(*Continued on next page*)

The Mystery of the Purple Pirate
The Mystery of the Wandering Cave Man
The Mystery of the Kidnapped Whale
The Mystery of the Missing Mermaid
The Mystery of the Two-Toed Pigeon
The Mystery of the Smashing Glass
The Mystery of the Trail of Terror
The Mystery of the Rogues' Reunion
The Mystery of the Creep-Show Crooks

FIND YOUR FATE™ MYSTERIES

The Case of the Weeping Coffin
The Case of the Dancing Dinosaur

PUZZLE BOOKS

The Three Investigators' Book of Mystery Puzzles